STAR WARS

THE LAST JEDI

by Michael Kogge

Based on the screenplay by
Rian Johnson

EGMONT

EGMONT
We bring stories to life

First published in Great Britain 2018
by Egmont UK Limited, The Yellow Building,
1 Nicholas Road, London W11 4AN

© & ™ 2018 Lucasfilm Ltd.

ISBN 978 0 6035 7513 6
70047/1

Printed in UK

To find more great *Star Wars* books, visit
www.egmont.co.uk/starwars

A long time ago in a galaxy far,
far away....

*The FIRST ORDER reigns. Having
decimated the peaceful
Republic, Supreme Leader Snoke
now deploys his merciless
legions to seize military
control of the galaxy.*

*Only General Leia Organa's small
band of RESISTANCE fighters stand
against the rising tyranny,
certain that Jedi Master Luke
Skywalker will return and restore
a spark of hope to the fight.*

*But the Resistance has been
exposed. As the First Order
speeds toward the rebel base,
the brave heroes mount a
desperate escape....*

PROLOGUE

ONCE there was a boy who grew up to become a Jedi Knight. Not just any Jedi, but one of the greatest in their history, a valiant hero who toppled an evil empire.

He was also the last of their kind.

For over a thousand generations, the Jedi Knights had been the guardians of peace and justice throughout the galaxy. With their connection to the Force, they could perform astonishing feats, influence minds, and perceive glimpses of what was and what might be. Yet for all their foresight, the Jedi failed to foresee their own future. One of their order turned against them, hunting down the other Jedi until their numbers were few and their light was all but extinguished.

The boy knew none of this growing up. What he did know was the barren desert of his home, where water was more valuable than gold.

He had a happy childhood. His aunt and uncle raised him on their moisture farm, and he was their son in all but name. His uncle could be cranky, but taught him everything from fixing vaporators to flying airspeeders, and his aunt was warm, spoiling him when she could. Like many boys his age, he was impatient, curious, and a bit brash. He had a talent for tinkering and a passion for speed.

He also had dreams.

On evenings after he'd finished his chores, he would go out and watch the binary sunset. The twin suns would descend below the dunes, one blazing white-hot, the other orange-red. Cast in the amber light, the boy would wonder about himself, who he was, where he would go, what he would become. He dreamed of getting off his dull and dusty homeworld and training to be a pilot, so he could sail through the depths of space, so he could see the stars.

He dreamed of being like his father.

What little the boy knew of his father he had learned from his uncle, in snatches and grumbles. Supposedly, his father had been a navigator on a spice freighter, yet something tragic had happened. His uncle had never elaborated, insisting the boy quit daydreaming and accept life on the homestead. There was no shame in being a moisture farmer. No shame at all.

Years passed, and this boy was now an old man. He stood on a cliff overlooking a great sea. He wore sackcloth robes under a woolen cloak. A hood protected his face from the wind. The water before him stretched to the horizon like the dune seas of his home, broken only by mountainous islands.

He had come to this forgotten world to retire in solitude. All his dreams he had fulfilled long before. He had flown the depths of space, seen the stars and all the light and dark between. He had nothing more to give and desired nothing in return. He just wanted to be left alone, in peace.

But after many years, he had been found.

He turned slowly from the sea. A girl stood on the other side of the plateau.

She approached but stopped within a few paces of him. He hesitated before he reached up with his hands—one of flesh and blood, the other of metal and wire—and pulled down his hood. For a long moment, he and the girl beheld each other, quiet with their own thoughts.

She had dark brown hair, braided in triple buns. Her vest and tunic were the color of sand. Gauze was wrapped around her arms, and her trousers were short, exposing fair skin above leather boots. She carried a quarterstaff that appeared salvaged from a gear axle. A worn canvas satchel dangled from her hip. Freckles dotted her face.

She slung the strap of her staff over her shoulder and opened her satchel. From that she removed a chrome cylinder about half the length of her arm. It was the hilt of a lightsaber. She held it out to him.

He inhaled deeply, and trembled.

This lightsaber had once belonged to him, and to his father before him. He had lost the weapon when he had lost his hand, during a fateful duel in a city among the clouds. He had thought it gone, forever, yet somehow it had been found, as had he.

He clenched his jaw and frowned. He did not take the lightsaber from her.

Her grip on the device wavered. She blinked. Her confusion gave way to distress. Yet still she held the hilt out to him. She wanted him to have it. She pleaded with her gaze.

The man's frown broke. His eyes moistened. The light-saber carried so many memories. Too many. He shouldn't accept it. Not now. Not after so long.

His metal fingers touched the hilt and took it from her.

The man stood there, near the edge of the cliff, considering the lightsaber in his grasp. It felt as light and familiar as it had the first time he had held it, back when he was around the girl's age. The old hermit who had given it to him said his father had built the lightsaber and had wanted his son to have it, but the boy's uncle wouldn't allow it.

That day, so long before, was the day his life had changed. It was the day he no longer had only dreams. It was the day he suddenly had a destiny.

Holding the hilt now, part of him wished he had never held it at all.

With a swift snap of his wrist, the man flung the light-saber off the cliff, toward the sea.

CHAPTER
1

"THEY'VE found us!" shouted a tactical officer.

On the bridge of the Resistance cruiser *Raddus*, Poe Dameron stood with General Leia Organa and her protocol droid, C-3PO, whose coverings had been recently buffed to a bright and shiny brass. But there was nothing bright or shiny in what captured their attention. Above a communications table the holograms of three dark-hulled warships blinked into existence, setting off alarms and panic across the bridge.

Admiral Ackbar, the Mon Calamari military genius who had directed the Rebel Alliance's triumph at Endor, manipulated the table's controls with his webbed hands. Two of the warships were identified as First Order Star Destroyers, the *Fellfire* and General Hux's flagship, the *Finalizer*. The other was the massive cannon-laden Dreadnought *Fulminatrix*.

"Well, we knew that was coming," Poe muttered.

The Resistance had recently obtained intelligence about the First Order's fleet from a pair of battle-hardened spies. Not only did the data include detailed schematics of the

Dreadnought, it showed that the enemy's navy was much larger than anyone had estimated. Anticipating the First Order would retaliate for the destruction of Starkiller Base, the Resistance leadership had begun the evacuation of their secret headquarters on D'Qar in earnest. But what no one had foreseen was how quickly the First Order would locate their hideout.

Poe pressed the transceiver button on the table. "Connix, is the base fully evacuated?"

Lieutenant Kaydel Ko Connix's image appeared on a monitor. Her long blond hair was knotted in side buns, and her natural smile wavered under stress. "Still loading the last batch of transports," she said. "We need more time!"

A glance out the viewport showed freighters, transports, and personnel shuttles rocketing away from the green orb of D'Qar. All headed toward the *Raddus* or one of the three other capital ships that made up the Resistance's meager starfleet: the spindly hospital frigate *Anodyne*, the bunker buster *Ninka*, and the cargo hauler *Vigil*. But it was clear that many wouldn't make it to safety, since they lay in the firing range of the Destroyers and Dreadnought.

Poe wished he were out there in his X-wing defending the evacuees instead of stuck on the bridge as a spectator. The mechanics had just mounted a souped-up booster engine to his starfighter and there seemed no better time than the present to put it to use.

Poe turned to General Organa. She was the last living princess of Alderaan and had witnessed firsthand her homeworld's annihilation by the Empire's Death Star. Her hair was rolled in a neat tuck and she wore a regal mantle over a plain silk gown, both in black. If not for the color of her dress, Poe never would have known she was mourning the death of her husband, Han Solo. He could only imagine the heartache she was hiding under her poise.

"You've got an idea," she said to him, "but I won't like it." She didn't make him explain himself. "Go."

Poe issued a remote command to his astromech, BB-8, from his wrist comm and rushed to the cruiser's hangar. When he got there, BB-8 was already secured in the socket of Poe's X-wing, *Black One*. Poe climbed into the pilot's seat. "Let's roll."

The starfighter shot out of the cruiser's hangar, its S-foils clamped and wings closed for maximum velocity. Poe called up an overview of the *Fulminatrix* on his cockpit display. Larger than the other vessels, the Dreadnought resembled three Star Destroyers welded atop each other in the form of a sinister, three-layered spearpoint. Turbolaser guns along its upper hull turned toward the Resistance fleet in orbit while the huge autocannons on its belly began to charge with energy. Poe's job was to stall the Dreadnought from firing those autocannons at D'Qar until the evacuation of the base was complete.

He flew straight toward the warships. BB-8 squawked his displeasure, which the X-wing's computer translated as he had a bad feeling about this.

"Happy beeps, buddy. We've pulled crazier stunts than

this," Poe said. While that might be true, he also knew one hit from a turbolaser and they'd be goners. "Happy beeps," he repeated, to calm his own nerves.

"For the record, I'm with the droid on this one," General Organa said over the private comm channel.

"Thanks for your support, General," Poe replied, amused that she was listening to his in-flight chitchat. But that was what made her an exceptional general. Her eyes and ears were everywhere, never missing a detail.

C-3PO's network of spy droids had reported that the head of the First Order's military, General Hux, had survived the destruction of Starkiller Base. With Poe out and about, it was time to see if that intelligence was indeed correct. Poe signaled the *Finalizer* in a subspace broadcast. "Attention! This is Poe Dameron of the Republic fleet. I have an urgent communiqué for General Hugs," he said, intentionally mispronouncing the general's name.

No response came. The X-wing continued its approach and would soon be in the warship's firing range. BB-8 gibbered anxiously. Poe was about to agree that maybe this wasn't the best idea after all when a pompous voice replied to his hail. "This is General Hux of the First Order. The Republic is no more. Your 'fleet' is rebel scum. Tell your precious princess there will be no surrender."

Following his plan, Poe pretended he hadn't heard the threat. "Hi, I'm holding for General Hugs."

"This is *Hux*! You and your friends are doomed. We will wipe your filth from the galaxy!"

Poe continued his charade. "Okay, I'll hold."

He waited. Clicks echoed over the comm. "Can you . . . Can he hear me?" Poe heard Hux ask someone on his bridge.

Black One was getting closer and the warships still hadn't fired. Poe's plan might work if he dragged out the conversation a little longer. "Hugs—with an *H*. Skinny guy. Sallow."

"I can hear you. Can you hear me?" Hux sounded irritated.

Poe's range counter neared zero. "I can't hold forever. If you reach him, tell him Leia has an urgent message for him." He wished Hux could see his smirk. "About his mother."

BB-8 trilled in glee. Poe had to hush him to hear the confusion from the *Finalizer*'s command staff. "I believe he's tooling with you, sir," said one of Hux's advisors.

"Open fire!" Hux yelled.

Poe cut the connection and grabbed his flight yoke. "Beebee-Ate, punch it!"

Its newly installed booster engine blazing, *Black One* tore past the *Finalizer* toward the *Fulminatrix* and opened its S-foils into attack position. The Dreadnought's turbolasers erupted immediately. Poe weaved the X-wing through the fire and dove close to the *Fulminatrix*'s hull, making his fighter a difficult target to hit.

He switched the comm to a friendly frequency and initiated the next stage of his semi-improvised plan. "Taking out the cannons now. Bombers, start your approach!"

Eight Resistance bombers, resembling atmospheric weathervanes with tubular fuselages, sped toward the Dreadnought from the opposite angle of Poe's approach. A score of X-wings and wedge-shaped A-wings surrounded the bombers as a starfighter escort.

"Bombers, keep that formation tight. Fighters, protect the bombers," commed Tallie Lintra, a former cropduster who flew the lead A-wing. "Let's do some damage and buy our fleet time."

Poe skimmed his X-wing over the Dreadnought's surface, blasting cannon after cannon to protect the bombers' approach. Since he flew under the firing arc of the guns, they were unable to hit him and proved easy targets to knock out. Poe had destroyed all except one cannon when BB-8 whistled a warning.

The X-wing's proximity sensors showed TIE fighters racing out of the Dreadnought toward the bombers. Painted mostly black, with two slim vertical wings connected to a circular cockpit, the TIEs were named after their twin ion engines, which gave them incredible speed. Though they lacked strong shields and had only two laser cannons compared with an X-wing's four, the TIEs' greatest assets were their pilots. They were afraid of nothing—not even death. To die in battle for the First Order was the greatest sacrifice a TIE pilot could make.

Three split off from the group to trail *Black One*. "Here comes the parade," Poe said.

Laser fire from the TIEs rattled his X-wing's underside,

where its shields were weakest. One lucky shot must have severed a power line to his cannons, because all of a sudden Poe couldn't return fire. "Beebee-Ate, my weapon systems are down. We need to take out that last cannon or our bombers are toast. Work your magic!"

Poe threw his X-wing into a series of barrel rolls, dodging enemy fire to give BB-8 a chance to weld the power line. A glance out the canopy showed the TIE squadrons were about to swarm the Resistance starfighters. "Tallie, heads up," he said.

"Gunners, look alive!" Tallie commed.

A-wings and X-wings engaged the TIEs while the bombers unleashed their turret guns. A brilliant display of laser bolts bloomed into a riot of fireballs. Dozens of TIEs met explosive ends, but the First Order still held the advantage with its greater numbers.

"They're everywhere! I can't—" said a pilot before his voice fizzled out.

Poe knew that voice. Good old Tubbs, who was always keen to mentor new fighter jocks. Now he was gone—as was the Candovantan ace Zizi Tlo. The TIEs had blown her A-wing to pieces.

"We're not going to get old out here, Poe," Tallie said. "Give me good news!"

"Hold tight!" Poe checked the status of his lasers. "Beebee-Ate, we gotta kill that last cannon. I need my guns!"

BB-8 carped back that the problem was in the hard-to-reach junction box. Repairs were going to take more time.

Poe evaded another enemy salvo, keeping the remaining turbolaser cannon in his sights. All he had to do was take it out so the bombers could safely drop their payloads on the Dreadnought and deal another major blow to the First Order.

But the *Fulminatrix* was determined to land its punch first. The two autocannons on its undercarriage belched a river of energy toward D'Qar. An explosion mushroomed where the Resistance base had been on the planet. Poe hoped no one was still down there.

Admiral Ackbar put to bed any such fears. "The last transports are aboard," the Mon Calamari gurgled in a wide broadcast. "Evacuation is complete!"

Poe let out a breath. Now all he had to do was destroy one last cannon and they wouldn't have to worry about the Dreadnought.

General Organa spoke over the private channel. "Poe, you did it. Now get your squad back here. We need to get the fleet out of here."

Poe couldn't believe what the general was saying. "No, we can finish this! How many chances do we get to take down a Dreadnought?"

"Disengage *now*—that's an order!"

Poe pretended not to hear her last command and clicked off the comm. She'd reprimand Poe for what he was about to do, but crippling the *Fulminatrix* would be worth any punishment. He swerved *Black One* around the TIEs that had been chasing him and squared the last cannon in his targeting computer. "Beebee-Ate—it's now or never!"

It had to be.

A clunk echoed in the innards of Poe's X-wing, but it was a good clunk. The weapons indicator on the cockpit console illuminated and BB-8 squealed in triumph. The little droid had done it. The X-wing's power conduit was welded and stabilized!

Poe didn't even wait for a full charge. He fired.

The Dreadnought's last active turbolaser exploded.

Straining against his seat straps, Poe wrenched his fighter around to confront his pursuers nose cone–first. So surprised were the TIE pilots by the oncoming X-wing that neither could trigger their lasers in time. Poe blasted them into stardust.

"All clear—bring the bombs!"

"Happy to!" Tallie replied over the comm.

Starfighters and bombers raced toward the Dreadnought. The bombers had been whittled down to half their original number, yet if even one managed to drop its payload of magno-charges on the Dreadnought, the damage inflicted could be devastating.

With its turbolasers disabled, the *Fulminatrix*'s defense rested with the TIE fighters, which increased by the minute as more launched from the Dreadnought and Destroyers. The leaders of the First Order viewed the TIEs as expendable and were willing to sustain heavy losses to overwhelm the Resistance ships.

The First Order's strategy seemed to be working. Screams crackled over Poe's comm as another bomber met its end. C'ai Threnalli, the tendril-mouthed Abednedo flying Red Three, yelled out in his native language, which the X-wing's computer translated as "We can't hold them!"

Poe took *Black One* into the fray. "Yes, we can! Stay tight with the bombers!"

One bomber in particular, painted cobalt blue, was giving the TIEs more than they could take. Salvo after salvo gushed from its undercannon, obliterating any TIE that came too close. Poe took heart in that gunner's dogged determination. It would spur everyone to keep up the fight more than any speech of his ever could.

CHAPTER
2

PAIGE spun in the turret seat of the bomber *Cobalt Hammer*, blasting at enemy fighters. Sweat trickled under the medallion on her neck. It was getting harder and harder to keep the TIEs away. Their numbers seemed endless.

"Almost there! Bombardiers, begin the drop sequence!" Tallie said over the bomber's speakers.

Releasing the magno-charges was Nix's responsibility as the bombardier of *Cobalt Hammer*. He was stationed at the top of the bomb bay, while Paige's turret was located at the bottom of the fuselage and faced backward to ward off any pursuers.

She continued firing, sending more TIEs to their doom. She didn't revel in any of it, knowing that each and every TIE was operated by someone like her.

The lead bomber *Crimson Smiter* zoomed past and opened its bomb bay door. "Sequence initiated," broadcast its bombardier. "Payload ready to del—"

His transmission never finished. A TIE careened into *Crimson Smiter*'s bomb bay and sparked a chain reaction.

All the bomber's magno-charges went off, spawning a destructive wave that swept through space.

Paige was rocked in her seat and her viewport went white. After the brightness dimmed, she saw the explosive wave had consumed not only the crimson bomber and the nearby TIEs, but all the other bombers.

Cobalt Hammer was the only bomber remaining.

Down below lay the sleek chrome of the Dreadnought's hull. But Nix would have to start dropping his payload soon. Sensors indicated that the Dreadnought's autocannons were rotating away from D'Qar to the Resistance cruiser *Raddus*, on which Paige's sister, Rose, currently served as a technician. She and thousands of others would die if the autocannons struck the cruiser.

A black X-wing sped under them. "*Cobalt Hammer*, why aren't your bay doors open?" came the voice of Commander Poe Dameron. "Nix, come in!"

When Nix didn't respond, Paige didn't wait for further instruction from Fossil, her commanding officer on the *Raddus*. She unbelted herself and crawled out of the turret into the bomb chute. Not one of the thousand magno-charges had been dropped. They all rested in their berths along the length of the shaft, and the bay doors below remained closed.

Smoke billowed down the chute. Paige crouched. Through the haze, she made out a body in a bombardier flight suit lying on the highest catwalk. "Nix? . . . *Nix?*"

The pilot didn't move. But an object in his hand blinked red—the bomb trigger remote.

"Drop the payload," Poe shouted over the bomber's speakers. "Now!"

Paige scuttled up a ladder to the catwalk. Poor Nix lay there, lifeless. The blast from the crimson bomber must have struck the upper part of *Cobalt Hammer*. She silently thanked Nix for managing to put the remote trigger within her reach.

The ship shook violently and Paige lost her footing. She fell off the ladder, down the chute, and smashed into a mid-level catwalk ten meters below.

Pain shot through her limbs. She could hardly move. The smoke thickened. She wheezed. TIEs must have hit the bomber again. Another barrage would probably destroy it for good.

Paige couldn't let that happen. People were depending on her. Her friends. Her family. Her little sister.

Rose would die if Paige didn't drop the bombs.

Paige turned her head to look up. Teetering on the edge of the catwalk, the remote shone through the smoke like a bright star on a cloudy night. The TIE fighter attack must have jostled it out of Nix's grip.

Paige kicked at the ladder. The upper catwalk shuddered, but the remote remained on the edge. She mustered her muscles for another kick. Her boots clanged against the ladder. The remote bounced, but didn't fall.

Smoke constricted her lungs. She couldn't even cough. "Now! Drop them now!" boomed Commander Dameron.

Paige gave one last kick. It had much less force than her other two attempts. But it was just enough to knock the remote off the catwalk.

It ricocheted off one bomb, then another, falling down the chute. Paige stretched out with every bit of strength left in her.

She caught the remote. The next action came naturally, ingrained from operating the turret. Her thumb pressed the remote's trigger.

A warning chimed, then the bay doors opened. From bottom to top, the racks retracted and the magno-charges tumbled from their berths. Down the chute they fell, a thousand black orbs, some painted with crude smiling faces or slogans like "Hi Snoke!", and each containing enough destructive power to level a village. They pelted the Dreadnought, erupting on contact, blasting chunks from its hull. Within moments, flames engulfed the *Fulminatrix* and everything around it—including *Cobalt Hammer*.

As fire washed over the bomber, Paige touched the medallion that hung around her neck and thought of Rose.

General Leia Organa did not join the cheering on the bridge of the *Raddus* when the Dreadnought broke apart. She couldn't celebrate the unnecessary sacrifices Poe Dameron had forced them to make. They had forfeited all eight bombers, along with most of the starfighter corps. The small

Resistance fleet might escape this time, but it would not be able to mount an ample defense when the First Order attacked again. And attack again it would, she knew. The First Order would not stop until the flame of the Resistance was snuffed out.

Her job was to ensure that never happened. "Light-speed," she said.

The bridge crew promptly resumed their duties and all the remaining ships in the fleet followed her command.

Rey?

Finn woke with a start—and banged his head against something hard. Wincing, he found himself lying inside a bubble bed, wearing a squishy suit from his neck to his toes. He retracted the dome and promptly fell off the bed onto the cold floor.

He was in a sick bay, far from the snowy forests of Starkiller Base where he remembered he had been fighting Kylo Ren, the First Order's black-garbed enforcer, in defense of his friend Rey. Relying on the advanced weapon training he'd received as a stormtrooper, he had managed to wield the lightsaber given to him by Maz Kanata and slash Kylo Ren in the arm. Incensed, Ren had lashed out with his own fiery blade, cutting deep into Finn's flesh before all went dark.

Finn felt an ache where Ren's saber had struck, but otherwise he seemed in good health. And if he had survived the encounter, it could mean that his friend had, too.

"Rey!" he called out. But there was no sign of her. He was alone.

The sick bay suddenly shook. Medical equipment fell off the shelves. Glow panels fluttered. Finn teetered up on uneasy legs. Sticky, icky bacta dripped from the tubes of his translucent body suit. The medicine had special properties that accelerated the healing process, but it was costly, even the synthetic blend the Resistance had acquired. His wound must have been quite severe for the Resistance to use its precious bacta on him.

He staggered out into a corridor. The walls gleamed white and were lined with access panels to circuitry and conduits. Engines hummed in the background. Finn figured he must be on a star cruiser.

"Rey?" he called again.

He peeked out a viewport and the dizzying streaks of hyperspace nearly made him sick. He turned away as a squad of soldiers in Resistance uniforms rushed past, paying him no attention, even in his current state of undress.

Finn didn't know what was going on, but he had to find Rey before things turned worse. He also had to find some clothes.

After landing inside the *Raddus's* hangar, Poe had BB-8 run a diagnostics program. *Black One* had sustained some hull damage in the combat, but nothing that couldn't be patched. Poe would recommend that the mechanics replace the power junction box, in case it failed again. As for the experimental booster engine, it had saved his skin, so he'd keep it.

Interrupting his tests, BB-8 twirled his dome and blabbed in excitement, beeping too fast for Poe to understand. "Finn naked? Leaking bag? Your chips all right?" Poe asked. Turning his head, he saw why the droid was so animated. Finn was bumbling around near the hangar door, looking very lost and wearing a translucent bacta suit.

Poe climbed out of his fighter and hurried over to his friend. "Buddy! It's good to see—" He stopped before he hugged the former stormtrooper. Gelatinous fluid was leaking from Finn's suit and had dribbled a trail on the ground. "Let's get you dressed. You must have a thousand questions."

Finn had but one. "Where's Rey?"

CHAPTER
3

HOPE.

Of all the shared beliefs in the universe, none was as outrageous—or as powerful. Born in the heart, not the mind, it blossomed in the bleakest of moments, inspiring courage when nothing else could. Logic and reason it defied. Faith and friendship it embraced. It was the antidote to despair, a sword for the soul, the last candle in the night. It was the lone voice that said there still might be a chance. Wrongs could be made right. The future remained untold. All was not lost.

For Rey and countless others, Luke Skywalker was the living embodiment of hope.

Decades before, when the Galactic Empire had imposed its tyranny on the galaxy, this farm boy from Tatooine destroyed the first Death Star and dethroned the Emperor. His bravery had stirred spirits across the galaxy, demonstrating that one person could make a difference, even in the darkest of times.

Yet as Rey looked at him standing on the cliff, holding

the lightsaber she had placed in his hand, there was something not quite right about him, something profoundly sad. The blue in his eyes had faded. Wrinkles burdened his brow. His hair was unkempt, peppered white and gray like his beard, and his robes were disheveled and grimy. It had probably been a long time since he had washed them—or himself.

His scraggly appearance didn't trouble Rey. He was still a Jedi and could teach her more about her special talents, which she could not control or comprehend by herself. And he could help save the Resistance from the First Order, as he had saved the Rebellion from the Empire. The galaxy needed Luke Skywalker to return.

But when he tossed his old lightsaber over the cliff without saying a word, Rey felt all her hopes fall with it.

He strode past her with barely a look, his robes swishing about him. She stood there, confounded. Had she made a mistake? Had she somehow insulted him? They hadn't even exchanged a word. All she'd done was present the lightsaber that had belonged to him, years before.

"Um . . . Master Skywalker?"

Rey followed him up the way she had come, then down the hill into what appeared to be a small settlement. Mounds of stacked stones formed primitive dwellings that bristled with lightning rods on the roofs. Luke walked into the biggest of these huts, then slammed the door behind him.

Rey paused at the hut. Perhaps a more formal introduction was in order. She rapped her knuckles on the metal door.

"Master Skywalker? I'm from the Resistance. General Leia sent me. We need your help. We need you to come back."

He did not answer. She knocked louder. "Hello?"

Again, he ignored her.

Leia had told Rey that her brother had become withdrawn since she'd last seen him, but Rey hadn't imagined he'd be so plain *rude*. In the old stories about him, he had always come off as sunny and sociable, a person who was friendly with everyone.

Rey remained there for some time, not knocking again. When it became obvious he wasn't going to come out or let her inside, she tried the door handle. It was locked.

Growing weary, she walked away. She thought about how she had gotten here, to this lonely island on this lost world. Weeks before, she had been scouring the desert for any scrap she could sell to buy her next meal. Since then, she had been on an adventure as incredible as anything from the old tales and had made new friends, one of whom she deeply missed. The last time she'd seen Finn, he lay in a coma, recovering from wounds he'd received defending her against Kylo Ren.

Rey's wanderings took her back to the cliff. She stopped where Luke had stood and stared out at the sea. It surrounded the island, vast and gray. Never in all her life had she seen so much water. Unlike the wastelands of Jakku, where salt burned her eyes and parched her throat, the briny smell of the sea refreshed her.

She looked around at the island. Who—or what—had

built the ancient staircase, the huts, or the stone wall that prevented the cliffs from eroding into the sea? It was all a mystery, as was most everything about this remote world, including the odd creatures on the cliff below her.

Thousands upon thousands of a small birdlike species had turned the cliff wall into a busy breeding ground. The most prominent of them flaunted orange head feathers and strutted around as if they were on display. Rey assumed they were the males, trying to attract the attentions of gray-colored females who by and large wanted nothing to do with them. Those in the colony not engaged in peacocking bumbled from rock to rock on webbed feet or nuzzled each other with wet snouts. Some nested, others perched, a few burrowed, and a couple flew, diving into the water to scoop up tiny fish. They reminded Rey of the bloggins on Jakku, though in place of eyestalks, these avians had round black eyes and appeared smarter simply by not running about willy-nilly. She doubted, however, that their feathers made soft pillows.

An object glinted on a grassy ledge partway down the cliff. Rey squinted. Could it be what she thought it was?

After testing her feet on the stones, she lowered herself down the stone wall. The descent was steep, the going slow. One slip and she would plummet to her death.

It took her a while to get down to the patch of grass. And there lay Luke's lightsaber, surrounded by a gaggle of the little animals. By some miracle, it had not fallen into the sea.

She gripped the wall with one hand and reached out with the other. The avians screeched and flapped away. She grabbed the lightsaber.

Leaning against the wall, she took a breath. Her fingers ached from the climbing. She massaged them, holding the lightsaber close.

A familiar shape caught her eye in a tide pool below. Submerged in the calm waters was an old X-wing starfighter, of the kind she had scavenged on Jakku.

Rey guessed it was Luke's, the X-wing he had flown during the Battle of Yavin, when he'd launched the proton torpedo that took out the Death Star. But the rust that rotted its frame indicated he had no intention of flying it again to leave the planet.

Rey would have to change those intentions if she was going to save her friends in the Resistance.

She returned to the bluff where she had landed the *Millennium Falcon*. Her copilot, Chewbacca, knelt on the top of the ship, his long hairy arms digging inside an open access panel. The classic-model astromech droid, R2-D2, stood below on his two hydraulic legs, offering encouraging beeps. But Chewbacca wasn't having any of it, growling in frustration.

"Chewie, what are you doing?" Rey asked the Wookiee. "I thought you'd taken out the compressor."

Chewbacca grunted back at her and yanked out a bunch of shredded cables. Having spent many lonesome nights on Jakku learning languages, Rey understood the basics of what he said. A pest had somehow wiggled under the *Falcon's* armor plating and was nibbling on the cables.

"Mynock?"

Chewbacca reached deeper into the cables and, with a yelp of pain, pulled out a member of the squat avian species she had seen on the cliff. Its feathers were coated in generator grease and it had latched its tiny mouth on to one of Chewbacca's fingers. The Wookiee howled and waved his arm to try to shake it off of him, but it wouldn't let go. Only when he was about to whack the creature against the panel did it release its hold. It fluttered on stubby wings and made a gentle landing near Rey. Instead of flying off, it waddled away toward the cliff.

R2-D2 tittered and Rey laughed. But her amusement ended abruptly when Chewbacca asked if Luke was coming to join them.

Luke Skywalker wanted to be left alone.

He'd come to Ahch-To for that purpose, to divorce himself from the rest of the galaxy once and for all. And after years of living here, he had foolishly convinced himself he was safe.

Yet he also knew that Leia would find him one day. She was his twin sister, after all, a Skywalker, strong in the Force. Stubborn, too—a woman who would not give up until she got what she needed.

Luke himself had grown stubborn over the years. He loved his sister, but he would stand his ground. For there was a reason Ahch-To's location had been hidden. The world held many secrets—secrets Luke had pledged to protect.

Inside his hut, Luke changed into a dark tunic and trousers and folded his Jedi robes in a storage chest. Once everything was neatly in place, he closed his eyes and relaxed. His worries began to vanish, one after another. Peace took hold.

A banging at the door broke his meditation, followed by the voice of the girl. "I'm with the Resistance. Your sister sent me and we need your help."

Luke's eyes flicked open. His irritation returned. "Go away."

The door rattled and, with a crack, broke from its frame. An enormous brown-haired Wookiee tossed the door aside and marched into his hut.

"Chewie?" Luke said. "What are you doing here?"

Chewbacca roared as Leia's young messenger entered behind him. "He said you're coming back with us," the girl said.

"I got that," Luke said, then addressed Chewbacca. "You shouldn't be here."

Chewbacca bellowed again, teetering toward anger. When enraged, Wookiees could become wildly violent. They had the strength to rip arms out of sockets if provoked.

Luke wasn't afraid. For all his ferocity, Chewbacca was a friend.

"How did you find me?" Luke asked.

The girl spoke for the Wookiee. "Long story. We'll tell you on the *Falcon*."

"The *Falcon*? Wait—" Luke craned his neck to glance out the doorway. No one else was out there. "Where's Han?"

Rey looked away from him. Chewbacca mewled. Their sadness said it all.

Han Solo was dead.

CHAPTER
4

A TURBOLIFT took Kylo Ren through the many levels of the Mega-Destroyer *Supremacy*. Clad all in black, with his mask, cape, helmet, and armor, he presented the image of strength. But it was his heart that his master would probe. It beat in his chest, hard as a stone.

The turbolift stopped and the grill of its doors parted. Kylo Ren strode out into the throne room of Supreme Leader Snoke.

A wide bridge led into a spacious chamber arched by steel supports. Dark crimson curtains shrouded the walls and windows. Mysterious purple-robed attendants, their eyes glowing under their hoods, lurked around a sophisticated oculus device that offered views of space. But what Ren took most notice of were the silent warriors who stood four abreast on each side of the room. Armed and armored in gleaming red, they seemed outfitted for ceremony, yet in actuality they were ready for combat at a moment's notice. These eight were the First Order's most elite fighters, the Praetorian Guards, and the various weapons they carried—pikes and polearms, vibro-voulges and electro-whips—could slice through the hardest metal or electrocute a being with a single lash. Ren respected them for their prowess, aware that as a group they could overpower him. Little respect, however, did he have for the ingrate of an officer who had arrived first. The meddlesome General Hux lingered before the throne, on which sat the Supreme Leader of the First Order himself.

Tall though he was, Snoke did not match the giant form he projected in hologram communications. Yet he did not need size to impose his will. The mere sight of him could terrify. For Snoke was a creature of skin and scar, a grotesque warping of life itself. Some great wound had split his bald head long before, and half his face and neck were melted in a twist of perpetual torment. Gold-flecked robes draped his gaunt frame while gold-threaded slippers swaddled his feet. When sitting, he leaned forward, his spine bent like a decrepit old hunchback. But age and appearance mattered little to Ren. All that mattered was the power Snoke could teach him.

General Hux walked toward the lift, smirking at Ren as he passed. It took every bit of Ren's self-control that he not choke the wretch. Hux may have rescued him from death on Starkiller Base, but that was only because the Supreme Leader had commanded it. Hux was the reason the First Order still lacked complete control of the galaxy. His poor leadership had cost them their superweapon and he deserved to be punished for it.

"Hux's plan seems to be working," Snoke said, his voice wet and oily. He always seemed to know what Ren was thinking. "The Resistance will soon be in our grasp."

At the turbolifts, Hux widened his snide grin. "Thank you, Supreme Leader."

Ren fumed under his mask. As long as Hux had Snoke's confidence, Ren couldn't touch him. But the instant Hux lost it, Ren would be there to strike him down—an act he would enjoy.

Hux entered the turbolift and the doors closed. Ren stepped forward and dropped to a knee before the throne.

"You wonder why I keep a rabid cur in such a place of power?" the Supreme Leader asked. "Mark this—a cur's weakness, properly manipulated, can be a sharp tool."

Ren said nothing. Whenever his master lectured, it was better simply to listen.

"How's your wound?"

This question demanded an answer, and Ren didn't flinch. "It's nothing," he said, his voice distorted. The electronic vocoder in his mask needed to be fixed.

Snoke snickered. "The mighty Kylo Ren. When I found you, I saw what all masters love to see. Raw, untamed power. And beyond that, something truly special—the potential of your bloodline. A new Vader."

The praise invigorated Ren. This was what he wanted from his master. This was the respect he deserved.

"Now I fear I was mistaken."

Ren's heart missed a beat. How could his master say that? Did he not know the deed he had done on Starkiller Base?

"I've given everything I have to you—to the dark side." He blinked moisture from his eyes. "Everything."

Snoke's voice hardened. "Take that ridiculous thing off. The mask."

The command infuriated Ren. He wore the mask to project the same soul-crushing fear that his grandfather, Darth Vader, had inspired during the glorious days of the Empire. Yet after all Ren had done to secure his master's favor, his efforts were mocked. And he hated his master for it.

Still, he obeyed.

Ren pulled off the helmet and unclasped the mask from his face. His skin was tender and raw underneath. Thick black sutures stitched the gash on his cheek that the girl had given him in their forest duel. He hadn't received bacta treatment in time to completely restore his skin. But the resulting scar would be a constant and painful reminder of what she had done to him. It would fuel his hate. It would motivate his vengeance.

Snoke bent down but didn't acknowledge Ren's wound. He touched Ren under his eye. "Yes, there it is." His spidery finger came up wet with a tear. Disgusted, he wiped it across Ren's face. "You have too much of your father's heart in you, young Solo."

Ren was about to explode. "I *killed* Han Solo! When the

moment came, I put my blade through him. I didn't hesitate!"

"And look at you. The deed split your spirit to the bone. You were unbalanced, bested by a girl who had never held a lightsaber. You failed."

Ren would take no more of his master's ridicule. His free hand dropped to the hilt of his lightsaber.

It never got close.

Bolts of electricity burst from Snoke's hands and coursed into Ren's body. Ren fell back, scorched and smoking.

Snoke relented and his Praetorians surrounded Ren, their various weapons pointed at him. "Skywalker lives. The seed of the Jedi Order lives. As long as it does, hope lives in the galaxy."

Twitching from the electrocution, Ren pushed himself back up, cradling his helmet in his arm. His master continued to belittle him. "I thought you would be the one to snuff it out. Alas, you're no Vader. You're just a child with a mask."

Ren refused to listen to any more. He spun on a boot and strode back across the bridge into the turbolift. He could feel his master's stare on his back, but he did not turn around.

When the lift doors shut, Ren bashed his helmet into the wall again and again. It dented and fractured. He imagined it was his master's head, turning to pulp. The fool would regret ridiculing him.

The lift stopped and the doors opened. A pair of First Order lieutenants chatted outside. Seeing Ren, they froze.

In their eyes, Ren saw the very fear he had wanted to

project. He didn't need a mask. These officers were afraid of him and his fury.

"Get my fighter ready," he barked and walked past them, flinging the pieces of his helmet at their feet.

The twin suns of Ahch-To bathed the village in the soft gold of afternoon. But the warm light gave little comfort to the three people seated outside the huts, especially Rey. The story she had begun with how she befriended Finn turned into tragedy as she revealed Kylo Ren's murder of his own father and her mentor.

"Han Solo was my friend," she said.

It was obvious Han had been the same to Luke Skywalker, even if they hadn't seen each other in years. The Jedi Master appeared shaken. Sitting next to him, Chewbacca moaned.

Rey returned to the purpose of her visit. "Leia showed me projections of the First Order's military. It's massive, and now that the Republic is destroyed, there's nothing to stop them. They will control all the major systems within weeks. They'll destroy the Resistance, Finn, everyone I care about. Will you help us? You have to help us," she pleaded. "We need the Jedi Order back. We need Luke Skywalker."

Luke's face hid nothing. Sadness was etched across it, but also wisdom and kindness. He was not someone who could turn his back on those in danger.

"No," Luke said.

Rey thought she had misheard him. "What?"

He rose from the ground. "You don't need Luke Skywalker."

Rey jumped up, wanting to howl at him. "Did you hear a word I just said? We really, *really* do!"

Her insistence got her nowhere with Luke. "You think, what, that I'm going to walk out with a laser sword and face down the whole First Order?" he asked. "The Jedi, if you had them back, a few dozen knights in robes, what do you think they would actually do?"

Rey recalled a phrase she had learned from the Jedi legends. "Restore the . . . balance of . . ."

Luke shook his head. "And what did you think was going to happen here? Do you think I don't know my friends are suffering, that I came to the most unfindable place in the galaxy for no reason at all?"

"Then why did you come here?" Rey snapped back.

Luke glanced at Chewbacca, who had remained quiet, as if he understood something about Luke that Rey did not. Then the Jedi bunched up his robes and headed to his hut, lifting the door back into its frame.

"I'm not leaving without you," Rey called after him.

CHAPTER
5

LEIA drank tea in her cabin on the *Raddus*, gazing at the swirls of hyperspace through her viewport. For the moment, the tunnel of light represented safety. Once the Resistance fleet returned to realspace, however, it would be vulnerable to attack. The rendezvous point in the remote Oetchi system would no doubt give them all a chance to regroup, but the Resistance's long-term survival depended on finding a secure place to rebuild and rally her Jedi brother to their cause. Without him, she knew they would never defeat the First Order.

She also missed Luke.

Leia had lost so much over the years—her homeworld, her parents, her Republic, her son, and most recently, Han, her husband. It seemed that everything she loved had been torn away from her to cause the most pain. She had endured it all, with little time to grieve. But how much could one person suffer? She needed her twin, now more than ever. She needed someone with whom she could talk and share her pain. Luke would understand.

Leia let the emotion pass through her. Many more beings had endured far worse catastrophes. She had to remain strong. The members of the Resistance were looking up to her, not her brother, to lead them in their struggle for freedom. They had answered the call to join her and she could not abandon them.

The safety of hyperspace broke apart into lines. Then the viewport showed a dark void, speckled with stars. General Leia Organa strode out of her cabin and headed to the bridge.

Poe came out from his quarters, his old flight jacket over an arm. BB-8 rolled beside him, Finn a step behind, putting on the shirt and trousers that Poe had lent him. Poe had gotten Finn up to speed on everything that had happened, but Finn had a million more questions. "So you blew up the Starkiller Base, Rey beat Kylo, the Resistance got the map—you won, right? Why does this not feel like winning?"

Poe led the way down the corridor toward the bridge. "We came out of hiding to attack Starkiller. It didn't take the First Order long to find our base."

"Look, Poe, I believe in what you guys are doing, but . . ." The former stormtrooper hesitated. "I didn't join this army. I followed Rey here. I just don't want you thinking I'm something I'm not."

Poe tried to reassure his friend with a smile. "It's gonna be all right. Don't worry. You're with us, where you belong."

He stopped and gave Finn his flight jacket. Finn had saved it from the TIE fighter crash on Jakku, and when they met again on D'Qar, Poe had told him to keep it. But when Finn was admitted to the medcenter, the jacket came back into Poe's possession. Hoping his friend would recover, Poe had tried to mend it as best he could, stitching combat patches over the tears and burn marks from Kylo Ren's lightsaber. "I'm not much of a sewer. Plus, I was, you know, saving the fleet."

Finn didn't seem as eager to accept the jacket as he had on D'Qar. Poe understood his wariness. Finn was still recuperating from nearly being killed. It might take him a while, but he'd eventually come around. He was a soldier, and soldiers never gave up the fight.

They rounded the corner and walked onto the bridge, where General Organa was inspecting a holographic star chart with Admiral Ackbar, Commander D'Acy, and other Resistance officers.

When Poe went up to her, she welcomed him with a slap to the face. "You're demoted."

Poe grimaced. He'd expected a reprimand, but never losing his rank. "For what, a successful run? We took out a Dreadnought!"

"At what cost? Pull your head out of your cockpit." She began to turn away from him.

Poe felt the need to defend himself. "You start an attack, you carry it through."

"There are things you can't solve by jumping in an X-wing and blowing something up. I need you to learn that."

"There were heroes on that mission," he said.

"*Dead* heroes," General Organa said. "No leaders."

She was a small woman, yet her words landed with tremendous force. He felt ashamed he had failed her, and any further explanation would be nothing more than an excuse.

During their argument, Finn had been studying the holographic star chart above the command table. Their present location appeared empty of stars and celestial bodies. "We're really nowhere. Deep space," he said. "How's Rey going to find us?"

General Organa pulled back her sleeve and revealed a black-corded bracelet adorned with aspherical metal device. It shone faintly.

"A cloaked binary beacon?" Finn asked.

The general smiled. "To light her way home."

Finn returned to the map. "So until she gets back, what's the plan?"

"We need to find a new base," the general said.

"One with enough power to get a distress signal to our allies scattered in the Outer Rim," suggested D'Acy. A career military officer, the tough-as-nails commander had seen her fair share of battles over the years.

"And most important, we need to get there undetected," General Organa added.

Emergency lights suddenly flashed. Sirens began to sound. "A proximity alert!" Ackbar shouted.

Poe couldn't stay quiet any longer. "That can't be—"

In the large viewport around the bridge, thirty First Order Star Destroyers emerged from hyperspace. One dwarfed them all, a thunderhead of a vessel. Veins of illumination ran along the kilometers of its surface to a central command area the size of a major metropolis. And it was armed with giant turbolaser cannons from bow to stern—on both sides.

It was Supreme Leader Snoke's flagship, the Mega-Destroyer *Supremacy.*

"You've got to be kidding me," Poe said. It made no sense that the First Order had found them so quickly. "Can we jump to lightspeed?"

Lieutenant Connix checked her readouts. "We have enough fuel for just one jump."

"Do it fast, we have to get out of here," Poe said, watching squadrons of TIE fighters launch from the Destroyers. If the Resistance fleet didn't jump soon, it would be swarmed.

"Wait." General Organa stared at the warships. "They tracked us through hyperspace."

"That's impossible," Poe said.

"Yes, it is," the general said. "And they've done it."

Poe didn't argue. Her explanation seemed to be the only possibility. First Order engineers had built the Starkiller superweapon, so it was conceivable they could invent a tracking device that transmitted through hyperspace.

Finn offered his own assessment. "So if we jump to lightspeed, they'll just find us again and we'll be out of fuel. We're trapped. They've got us."

"Not yet they don't." Poe turned to General Organa. "Permission to jump in an X-wing and blow something up."

She didn't hesitate. "Granted. Admiral, swing us around."

Cannon fire from the Mega-Destroyer rattled everyone on the bridge. Ackbar leaned a webbed hand on a console to maintain his balance. "Full astern! Rotate shields!"

Poe ran off the bridge, Finn a few steps behind him. More shots rocked the cruiser. The pattern of the blasts told Poe that some of the TIEs were already on them. BB-8 wheeled ahead of them, squealing that they needed to go faster.

"Don't wait for me!" Poe told BB-8. "Get in and fire her up!"

Poe followed the droid into the hangar. Tallie and the other pilots sat in the cockpits of their starfighters and prepared for launch.

The launch never happened.

Torpedoes from a First Order TIE fighter shot into the hangar and detonated. In the blink of an eye, fuel lines burst and the place erupted. Flames consumed every craft, from the A-wings to Poe's beloved *Black One*. Tallie was in her cockpit when it blew apart.

The force of the blast saved Poe and BB-8 from suffering the terrible fate of their comrades. Both were sent reeling backward into the corridor. BB-8's dome flew off the ball of his body, but he was able to activate his magnetic casters to reconnect it. The blast doors shut, sealing off the hangar to prevent the fire from spreading.

Finn dashed toward them. "Poe! Are you all right?"

Poe took his friend's hand and staggered to his feet. "We need to get out of range of the Star Destroyers."

The Resistance would not survive otherwise.

CHAPTER
6

VEERING away from the *Raddus* in his TIE silencer, Kylo Ren watched his torpedoes tear open the cruiser's hangar and decimate the starfighters within. The brilliance of the explosions dazzled him.

But he was not done. He wanted to take out more than a hangar full of starfighters. He wanted to eliminate the Resistance's leaders.

Ren looped his fighter around for another attack run, and the two black-and-red TIEs behind him did the same. Fast though they were, they struggled to keep up, for Ren had followed the example of his grandfather Darth Vader and flew a custom TIE. The silencer bore a sleek, sinister design, with an oblong cockpit, a squashed rectangular viewport, and two solar wings that were notched and slanted like those on an interceptor. It tore through space with unrivaled speed and packed weaponry as devastating as the Special Forces TIEs flying with it.

Closing in on the cruiser's bridge, Ren waited for a torpedo lock. Since he had annihilated the cruiser's starfighters in the hangar, he needn't worry about any A-wings or X-wings harassing him, and the turbolasers on the First Order's Destroyers were keeping the cruiser busy.

The targeting computer beeped. His fingers twitched, ready to fire—until a sensation in the Force made him hesitate. On that bridge stood someone once close to him, as close as anyone could or ever would be. A person who shared his stubbornness, tenacity, and defiance.

His mother.

He felt that Leia—or General Organa as her minions in the Resistance called her—sensed him too. She held no anger against him, despite what he had done, despite that he had killed his father and her husband. For some reason, she still cared for him, as if he hadn't changed, as if he were still Ben Solo, her son.

How dare she.

His anger fused into an emotional missile. He launched it at her through the Force, a bolt of pure rage. He felt her stagger back and it gave him joy. He wanted her to know his pain. He wasn't Ben Solo. He was Kylo Ren. And he would sever his bond with her once and for all.

But he didn't press the trigger. Something blocked him at the last moment—some twinge of guilt or deep-seated fear.

Nothing stopped the other TIE pilots from firing. A pair of mag-pulse warheads struck the cruiser's bridge and Ren felt a chorus of voices crying out in the Force before they went quiet.

Ren jerked his flight yoke, rolling his silencer to avoid

the debris. His breathing was strained. He might not have personally killed his parent this time, but the bond had been severed nonetheless.

He no longer felt his mother.

General Hux addressed him on the comm. "The Resistance has pulled out of range of our Destroyers. We can't cover you at this distance. Return to the fleet."

Ren's anger flared again. "No!" he snapped back. It would be folly to retreat when a couple more well-placed shots could destroy the cruiser. Other TIE squadrons had downed the cargo hauler *Vigil*. They could eradicate the fleet right here, right now.

Wounded though it might be, the *Raddus* wasn't going down without a fight. Its turbolasers nailed one of the TIEs flying beside Ren, blowing it to pieces.

"Snoke's command," Hux said on the comm. "They won't last long burning fuel like this. It's just a matter of time."

The cruiser's guns erased a second TIE from Ren's scopes. If he continued the assault without the Destroyers' protection, he and his squadron could all die. Then victory would be pointless.

He turned his silencer away from the cruiser and commanded the TIEs to do the same.

In a flash of light, Admiral Ackbar, the most esteemed military commander of his generation, was gone. Ackbar's number two, Captain Gawat, went with him, as did the rest of the bridge crew on the *Raddus*. Either they were vaporized in the explosion or sucked out into the vacuum of space.

Only Leia survived.

She drifted, arms spread, between burning fragments of the bridge. Her training in the Force allowed her to slow her breathing and retain some of her heat, but she would not last out here forever. She was being suffocated, deprived of oxygen. Soon she would join the rest.

Several TIEs and a fighter in the shape of a claw flew past the debris back toward the fleet of Star Destroyers. Her son had piloted that fighter—her wayward, vicious, vengeful son. Corrupted by Snoke, Ben had committed the most reprehensible acts of violence against the most innocent among them. And Leia felt responsible. All her life she had worked to guard the galaxy from evil, but she could not protect it from the evils of her own child.

And yet still she loved him.

She would've done anything to see Ben again, as Han had, if only for a moment.

The stars blurred. A chill bit into her bones. She readied herself for the end.

A light floated in front of her, circular in shape, like a micro-sized moon. It was her beacon. The bracelet had come loose from her wrist.

She took hold of it. Its soft light reminded her of Rey.

The beacon needed to be returned to the cruiser, else the girl might never find the Resistance to bring Luke back. And then every last hope would be extinguished.

Leia shut her eyes and dropped her head to her chest. She forgot about the cold in her bones and even her breath. Her sole focus was the Force.

She rode its currents back into the hole in the cruiser bridge.

Finn pushed himself up, groggy from the fall. The First Order attack had knocked him off his feet and into a bulkhead. He'd been chasing after Poe, but with the corridor branching ahead, he couldn't tell which direction Poe had gone.

Rounding the bend, he skidded to a halt. Crew were crowded around an open airlock, where droids were carrying out a stretcher. "Her life signs are weak, but she's fighting," a medic reported.

Poe stood among the crew, gesturing frantically. "Move back! Give room!"

Finn stepped to the side to let the stretcher pass. On it lay none other than General Leia Organa.

An object dropped from her hand and fell near Finn's feet. No one else noticed, so Finn picked it up. It was the wrist beacon that the general had showed him on the bridge.

He moved away from the crowd and examined the glowing beacon. Somewhere out in the wide galaxy, Rey had one, too.

CHAPTER
7

THE ISLAND was haunted. Rey was sure of it.

She stood outside Luke's hut and watched the fog roll across the village. The haze was thick and held an eerie pre-dawn glow. She had the vague impression that something lurked within those mists. Specters whispering secrets from a long-lost time.

Stay here. I'll come back for you, sweetheart. I promise.

The voice startled her. Those words were the same she had heard so many times in her dreams on Jakku. Yet this was not Jakku. And looking around, she saw she stood alone.

Shortly before sunrise, the fog dissipated and Luke emerged from his hut. He strode past Rey as if she weren't there. Strapped to his back was a rucksack, a staff, netting, and an assortment of other items. She didn't ask where he was going. She just followed.

She trailed him up the mountain, then down the other side to the shore where a blubbery, bovine creature lounged on the rocks. Luke climbed up to it and untied an empty bottle from his back. He then took the two teats that hung beneath the creature's stomach and milked them. A green fluid oozed into the bottle.

The creature turned its leathery neck to Rey. Above a tubular snout, two tiny black eyes peered at her. The milking seemed to comfort it.

After filling the bottle, Luke put it to his lips and drank. Green liquid dribbled from the bottle into his beard. He didn't wipe the slime away, nor did he offer a sip of the milk to Rey. She wouldn't have accepted anyway.

Once refreshed, he capped the bottle and returned to his hut, closing the door behind him. Rey sat on a bench outside. She reached into her satchel, shifting aside the beacon Leia had given her to take out a ration packet. It was a leftover quarter portion she'd traded with the disgusting Unkar Plutt for scrap metal on Jakku. The food tasted bland, but at least it was better than green milk. After she was finished, she put on her cloak and slept.

Before dawn the next day, Luke came out, again outfitted for travel. Rey followed him to the edge of a cliff. The bay below was calm, though on the horizon loomed a storm.

Luke grabbed a wooden pole that rested against the ledge. Long and thin, it extended all the way down into the water. Luke tested its strength, then to Rey's astonishment, used it as a lever to vault himself over the bay. After landing atop the cliff on the other side, he pulled the pole out of the shallows. Its end bore a sharp metal hook.

Rey watched as Luke surveyed the waters. Without warning, he shoved the spear back into the sea. When he lifted the pole again, a fish bigger than Rey was hooked on its end.

Luke shifted the pole to the rocky beach, where the fish flapped, its mouth tendrils wiggling. He leaned the pole against the ledge and walked down a path to the beach. Rey found a similar trail on her side of the cliff.

By the time she reached the fish, the storm had hit. Rain pummeled her and the wind shrilled. It was so harsh she threw on the hood of her cloak. She'd worn the garment only for Jakku's sandstorms, never once thinking she'd don it for rain.

The inclement weather appeared to refresh Luke. He hoisted the giant fish over his shoulders and hiked up the path Rey had taken down. As he had before, he ignored Rey. But she trudged after him through the driving rain, hood up, staff in hand.

Rey stayed outside the hut that night. She was drenched, her teeth chattering from the cold. She got barely a wink of sleep. When Luke emerged from his hut that morning, she stayed on the log. Her tired body wanted to keep resting.

As he walked past her, he paused. It wasn't for long, but it was enough. She found the strength to get up and stumbled after him.

Her strength flagged as they climbed a crumbling staircase. Slick stone made the going treacherous. One slip, and she'd fall off the cliff to smash on the rocks below.

When they neared the top of the staircase, the whispers began to speak to her again.

The morning haze had lifted, revealing the shrubbery and moss that greened the cliffside. No wind blew. Yet the whispers grew louder. They said nothing comprehensible, no promise as before, perhaps nothing at all. Was she hearing voices in her head?

She climbed a few more steps before she saw the tree.

It was a fortress of nature. Three pulpy offshoots stood guard around a gigantic central trunk. All had tops splintered like jagged crowns, and none bore foliage or branches. Only moss grew on the ashen bark. A wide gap in the trunk looked to be a portal into the tree.

Rey moved toward the gap. The whispers rose in volume, clearly emanating from the tree. She had seen the tree before, somewhere. Had it been in her dreams? Or in the vision that had come to her when she'd touched Luke's lightsaber in Maz Kanata's castle? She couldn't be sure. Those memories were muddled in her mind. It was hard to remember what was real and what wasn't.

She heard Luke stop behind her, but she did not glance back at him. She ducked through the gap and entered the tree.

The interior of the trunk had been hollowed out into a chamber. Strips of bark plastered the walls in intricate designs. There was no sign of rot, despite the damp conditions outside.

A strange illumination drew her focus. In an alcove surrounded by a sunburst pattern of bark rested a shelf of dusty books. They seemed to shine with a light of their own.

The whispers became a hum—not of voices but of energy. The books *called* to her.

She stepped closer to them. They weren't everyday datapads or electronic binders, but leather-bound tomes of flimsy and paper, like the journals she had kept on Jakku. She reached for one.

"Who are you?"

She turned at the sound of Luke's voice. He stood in the doorway, regarding her as if for the first time.

Fleeting memories guided her words. "I know this place," she said. "This is a . . . library."

Luke came forward. "Built a thousand generations ago, to keep the original Jedi texts, the foundation of the ancient faith." He removed a book from the shelf and opened it. "They were the first—and now, just like me—they are the last of the Jedi religion."

The elaborate runes that decorated the book's pages captivated Rey. They were mysterious and yet familiar at the same time.

"You know this place," Luke said. "You've seen these books. You've seen this island."

"Only in dreams," Rey said.

Luke narrowed his eyes at her. "Who are you?"

It was the question she'd often asked herself. All she could say for certain was the purpose for her visit to Ahch-To. "The Resistance sent me."

"If they sent you, what's special about you? Jedi lineage? Royalty?"

She wished she was special or a Jedi or royalty. Maybe then he would listen to her. But she didn't dare reveal what she actually was.

"An orphan," Luke said, reading into her silence. "Where are you from?"

"Nowhere."

"No one's from nowhere."

She sighed. "Jakku."

A hint of a smile tugged the corners of his mouth. "All right, that is pretty much nowhere. Why are you here, Rey from nowhere?"

"The Resistance sent me. We need your help. The First Order—"

Luke's smile vanished. "Why are you here?"

Rey diverted her eyes. She knew what he meant. There was a reason Leia had sent her and not Poe Dameron or someone more qualified for secret missions. Leia had recognized Rey's extraordinary gifts.

"Something inside me has always been there, but now it's"—she paused, grasping for the right word—"*awake*. And I'm—I'm afraid. I don't know what it is or what to do, and I need help. I need someone to show me my place in all of this."

"You want a teacher."

For a moment, her hopes returned—but like a spark, they fizzled out when Luke spoke again. "I can't teach you."

"Why not? I've seen your daily routine. You're not busy."

"I'll never teach another generation of Jedi," he said.

She shook her head. This was Luke Skywalker, the icon of the Rebellion, who had defeated Death Stars and the Emperor and had single-handedly resurrected the Jedi Order from its ashes. How could he give up on what he had spent the greater part of his life building?

Luke stepped back to the doorway and leaned a hand against the trunk. "You asked why I came here? I came to this island to die, and to make sure the Jedi Order dies with me."

He stared out at the island, then looked back at her. "I know only one truth," he said. Conviction knit his brow. "It's time for all of this to end."

His defeatism startled her. "Why?"

"You can't understand."

"Make me. Leia sent me here with the hope you'd return. If she was wrong, she deserves to know why. We all do."

Luke responded by walking out of the library, leaving her alone. Sadly, she had been right. The island was haunted. The great Luke Skywalker, Master of the Jedi, was but a ghost of the hero he once had been.

Finn slumped down in a corridor on the *Raddus*. Crew rushed past, occasionally glancing at him as if he should be doing something. But what could he do? The cruiser had lost its starfighters, so there was no need for his rather poor gunnery skills. And he knew nothing about repairing starships. The First Order had trained him to excel on the battlefield, not in engineering.

The beacon he held continued to emit its warm glow. Did the light mean that Rey was still alive? General Organa hadn't explained the details. All Finn knew was that the beacon would lead Rey back to the cruiser—and right now, that was too risky with the First Order on their tail. She'd likely be captured or killed. Even if Skywalker returned with her, Finn doubted that anyone—Jedi or not—could survive an attack from thirty Star Destroyers.

Everything seemed doomed. And all he could do was stare at the floor.

BB-8 roamed the hallway, halting before Finn. The droid bobbed his dome to the right and left, looking at Finn and beeping in concern, but Finn didn't lift his head. He wasn't in the mood for a pep talk, especially from this particular astromech. He was about to tell BB-8 to scram when the droid's projector switched on and a holographic recording flickered before him.

In the Resistance's medical center on D'Qar, Rey stood over Finn as he lay in a coma. She looked at him for some time, then leaned over his recovery pod and kissed his forehead. "We'll see each other again. I believe that," she said. "Thank you, my friend."

The hologram vanished. Dust motes floated in Rey's place. A few moments passed before Finn's heart settled down. "Kinda weird you recorded that, but . . ."

His gaze fell to the beacon in his grasp. It seemed to shine brighter than before. "Thank you," he told BB-8. "I know what I've got to do."

The droid burbled, then rolled away. Finn didn't putter around either. He got to his feet and rushed down the corridor.

If it was too dangerous for Rey to come to them, he would find a way to go to her.

Luke's meditation that evening took him into his memories, to a time prior to his attempt to restore the Jedi Order. He had been a young man, little more than twenty years old, when on Dagobah he happened upon another tree that held secrets. It emanated an energy that Luke had not felt before, like a chill in the Force. A domain of evil it was, or so said his master at the time.

"What's in there?" Luke asked.

"Only what you take with you," his master said.

As Luke stepped toward the tree, his master remarked that his weapons weren't needed. Luke took them anyway.

The bole of the tree led him down into a cave, cold and slimy and smelling of death. Snakes, lizards, and other scaly creatures slithered between the branches and vines. He trod past them, carefully going deeper into the cave. And then out of the darkness emerged a figure armored all in black, the killer of both his first teacher, Obi-Wan Kenobi, and allegedly his father, Anakin Skywalker: the villain known as Darth Vader.

Luke ignited his lightsaber first. Vader followed with his, red against Luke's blue. The Dark Lord spared no words in that fight, and Luke never forgot the sound of Vader's mechanical respiration. Luke won the duel by landing a furious blow to Vader's helmet. When the helmet fell from Vader's body and rolled in the muck, its mask exploded, revealing a face underneath—a face that was none other than Luke's.

Soon after their encounter in the cave, Luke had fought Vader again, not as a phantom but in the flesh in Cloud City. There the Dark Lord had uttered words behind his rasping breaths, providing an answer to the mystery of the cave. He revealed he had not murdered Luke's father as Obi-Wan had told Luke.

He *was* Luke's father.

Luke had screamed in denial. No, no, it couldn't be true. It was impossible.

Yet it *was* possible. And it *was* true. It was a secret he had taken with him into the cave. A secret that had revealed itself when he saw his own face in Vader's helmet. A secret about his father that he had somehow always known, even if it had been withheld from him growing up.

Kids know.

Rey also knew the secret of her parents, if she would admit it. But she had buried her secrets deep and walled herself against them. It was as if she feared such secrets could destroy her.

Luke could not teach someone as guarded as her. He had tried to do so before, and he had failed.

CHAPTER
8

PAIGE'S death hit Rose hard.

The young technician took refuge in a utility corridor on the *Raddus*. The initial shock she'd felt learning what had befallen Paige's bomber had spiraled into grief. Her older sister meant everything to her. Paige was the person Rose had admired since her first memory. The two had spent their childhoods together, suffering through the First Order's brutal takeover of the mining colony where they grew up, looking out for each other in those dark hours, yet also trading joys and laughs and secrets only sisters could share.

Rose sniffled and stared at the old phase-band ring that the bomber squadron commander, a stout, silvery Martigrade named Fossil, had given her to honor her sister's sacrifice. What looked like an ornate ring could, by the switch of a tiny lever, iris open to reveal the starbird crest of the Rebel Alliance. During the rule of the Empire, senators had worn rings such as this to hide their loyalty to the Rebellion. The historical significance of this gift would have deeply affected Paige.

But history and politics were least on Rose's mind. She

could only think of Paige. How she would never hug her sister again when she returned from a mission. How the two of them would never adopt a pet together or get to ride a Pamaradian prancer or a fleet-footed fathier. How they would never talk, just *talk*, like they could for hours, sometimes about what was going on, sometimes about nothing at all.

Rose touched the only other piece of jewelry she owned, a medallion of Haysian smelt that hung from a necklace. It was the shape of a half crescent and engraved with the emblem of her home. Paige had worn a medallion just like it. Their matched pair represented the double-planet system of Otomok, containing Hays Major and Hays Minor, their homeworld. It also signified the closest of bonds between Rose and her older sister. They were like planets orbiting each other.

Except that now they weren't. Now one of the planets was gone.

The echo of footsteps told Rose that someone was near. But who else would come down here? All the other engineers were engaged in repairs elsewhere on the cruiser.

Rose wiped away her tears with her sleeve and stood. She tiptoed to the corner and peeked around it, spying a young man in a patched-up flight jacket. He opened the hatch of an escape pod and threw the sack he carried inside.

"What are you doing here?" she asked.

At the sound of her voice, the young man knocked his head against the hatch. He turned, pretending it didn't happen. "Hi. I was, umm, just doing a—"

"No, what are *you* doing here, down in maintenance?"

Rose moved a little closer. She recognized him from somewhere. "You're . . . *Finn!*" She blushed. She should've identified him at first sight. Anyone who followed galactic events knew who this young man was. "*The* Finn!"

"The Finn?" he repeated.

"I'm sorry for being an idiot, it's just, I'm not an idiot, I work behind pipes all day and talking with Resistance heroes is not my forte and, oh, I'm Rose and—"

"Breathe," he said.

It was exactly what Paige would've said. Rose quit talking and breathed. It calmed her down, but she felt even more embarrassed. She had the tendency to jabber on like an excited astromech.

"I'm not a Resistance hero," Finn said. "But it was nice meeting you, Rose."

He stood in the threshold of the escape pod, looking at her. He wanted her to leave. "Okay," she said.

She retreated into the utility corridor. If only she could tell her sister! Finn was so charming and courageous and—

She turned back into the hallway just as he was about to duck into the pod. "But you *are* a hero and that's important. You left the First Order, and what you did on Starkiller Base—"

"Listen—"

Rose talked over him. "When we heard about it, Paige—that's my sister—said, 'Rose, that's a real hero. Know right from wrong, and don't run away when it gets hard.'" She took another breath, glad to get it all out.

"Sure" was all Finn said in reply.

His nervousness perplexed her, though it was also possible he was just taken aback. She had that effect on people. "You know, just this morning I've had to stun three people trying to jump ship in these escape pods, running away." She pulled out her electro-shock prod and waved it around to demonstrate.

Finn leaned away and frowned. "That's terrible."

"I know. Anyway . . ." Her excitement began to wane as she reconsidered the situation. Why was someone of his stature in maintenance? Shouldn't he be advising the other officers?

"Well, I should get back to . . ." he said, fidgeting, "what I was doing."

"What *were* you doing?"

"Checking. Just checking the . . . ah . . . doing a check," he stuttered.

She glanced past him into the pod, at the sack he'd tossed inside. "Checking the *escape pods*?"

Finn nodded. "Routine check."

"By boarding one? With a *packed* bag?" she asked.

"Okay. Listen—"

His hemming and hawing didn't sound like what a hero would say. He sounded like a deserter.

Rose jabbed her electro-shock prod at him. Its high-voltage discharge could fuse broken circuits and shock a human deaf and dumb.

It sent Finn tumbling into the wall.

Poe and the surviving members of the Resistance leadership sat in the tight space of the *Raddus*'s emergency bridge. Commander D'Acy, who had been on an errand when the attack destroyed the main bridge, addressed the assembled. "General Organa—*Leia*," she said, with reverence, "is unconscious but recovering. That's the only good news I have. Admiral Ackbar, the rest of our leadership—they're gone. Leia was the sole survivor on the bridge."

Standing near Poe, C-3PO sounded like he was caught in a loop. "Oh dear, oh dear . . ."

"If she were here," D'Acy said, "she'd say save your sorrow for after the fight. To that end, she left clear instructions as to who should take her place. Someone she's always trusted, who has her full confidence."

Poe straightened in anticipation. Though they had their differences, Leia had always recognized his dedication to the Resistance. He would be proud to accept any leadership role on her behalf.

"Vice Admiral Holdo, of the cruiser *Ninka*," D'Acy said and stepped back.

The choice was such a surprise to Poe that he didn't know whether he felt crushed or grateful he wasn't picked. He had never met the vice admiral in person, but he had heard that she and General Organa had been friends since youth. He also knew she was recognized as a great strategic mind, admired even by Ackbar.

"Thank you, Commander." Dressed in a slender gown

and neck wrap a few shades darker than her purple hair, Vice Admiral Amilyn Holdo bore herself with dignity and grace. "Look around you. There are four hundred of you on three ships. We are the last of the Resistance, but we are not alone. In every corner of the galaxy, the downtrodden and oppressed know our symbol and they put their hope in it. We are the spark that will light the fire that will restore the Republic. That spark—this resistance—must survive. That is our mission."

Her voice conveyed a quiet strength. Everyone on the bridge hung on to her words, including Poe.

"To your stations, and may the Force be with us."

Poe blinked. That was it? She hadn't given them any instructions. Yet no one else seemed puzzled.

Poe leaned over to C'ai Threnalli, who was sitting next to him. "That's Admiral Holdo? Battle of Chyron Belt Admiral Holdo?"

The Abednedo mumbled an affirmative.

"Not what I expected," Poe said. A great military strategist should have formulated something more than a speech.

As the others disbanded, Poe approached Holdo and saluted. "Vice Admiral, Commander Dameron. With our current fuel consumption, there's a very limited amount of time we can stay out of range of those Destroyers."

"Very kind of you to make me aware."

"And we need to shake them before we find another base," he said. "What's our plan?"

She rebuffed him immediately. "Our plan, Captain? Not

commander, right? Wasn't it Leia's last official act to demote you? For your Dreadnought plan, where we lost our entire bomber fleet?"

"Captain, commander, you can call me whatever you like, I just want to know what we're doing," Poe said.

"Of course you do. I understand—I've dealt with plenty of trigger-happy flyboys like you. You're impulsive. Dangerous. And the last thing we need right now."

Holdo wasn't being sarcastic. She was being serious. Poe couldn't contain his shock. "Leia put the Resistance in your hands? Do you even have a plan?"

"Captain Dameron, that is need-to-know information, and you do not need to know. Stick to your post and follow my orders." She turned her back to him and went to a console.

Poe froze, unsure of what he should do. BB-8 rolled around him, trying to buoy his spirits, but he needed something more than reassuring beeps. He needed wisdom and advice.

He needed General Organa.

CHAPTER
9

LUKE flipped up the hood of his cloak and slipped out of his hut. It was the dead of night.

Rey snored on an outdoor bench, too deep in sleep to notice him. He ascended the hill, then crossed the island in the moonlight. Wookiee growls led him to the landing site of the *Millennium Falcon*.

Chewbacca roasted his dinner outside the ship. He grabbed a spit from the campfire and brought the blackened slab on it to his lips. Before he bit into the meat, an uncooked member of its species, one of Ahch-To's little avians, waddled up from a group and stared at him innocently. Chewbacca snarled, showing fangs, and the other avians around him shot in all directions, much faster than they appeared capable of moving.

The Wookiee returned to eat his meal, but then dropped it with a guilty whine. Luke smiled as he walked up the *Falcon*'s boarding ramp. Chewbacca's heart always won out over his hunger.

The interior of the ship hadn't changed much since

Luke's first trip off Tatooine in it. Grease stained the bulkheads. Loose plates rattled on the floor. Rust ate at the rungs of the turret ladder. Frayed wires spilled out of a wall socket. None of it concerned Luke. The *Falcon* wouldn't be the *Falcon* if it wasn't in a perpetual state of disrepair.

In the cockpit, the pilot's seat still showed Han's contours, worn in from decades of use. Luke gripped its edge and looked out the canopy at the night sky. Gold six-sided chance cubes dangled from the canopy near Chewbacca's chair. Luke held them with his metal fingers, detecting an almost imperceptible weight on one side of the cubes that most certainly favored landing on the sixes.

He entered the lounge where Obi-Wan Kenobi had trained him how to wield a lightsaber. The blast helmet he'd worn to cover his eyes while fighting the remote rested on a shelf, probably untouched since that test. The holographic chessboard, however, had seen much more recent use. Its console lights blinked for a saved game to be resumed.

Luke sat down on the couch, remembering the moments he'd had on this ship. A series of gentle electronic beeps—more familiar to him than any other sound in the universe—told him he wasn't alone. "Artoo?"

The silver-domed astromech unit wheeled out of a corner. Though the droid had a little rust around the edges, none of that stopped him from squealing at seeing Luke and venting disappointment that his old master had left him behind.

"Yes, yes, I know." But Luke's concession didn't stop the droid from blurting out binary Luke knew he had never programmed. "Hey—sacred island. Watch the language."

R2-D2 switched his vocabulary, but not the forceful tone of his beeps. The droid wanted Luke to return and help the Resistance.

"Old friend, I'm doing what's best. Nothing can change my mind." Luke touched the astromech's dome, as he had so many times in the past. It was a human gesture, but it usually had the effect of calming down the short-fused droid.

R2-D2 quieted, as Luke had hoped he would. Yet in place of beeps, the droid projected a hologram—the same hologram he'd projected when Luke had first encountered the droid more than forty years before on Tatooine.

Luke's twin sister, Leia, leaned before him in miniature, making a silent plea. She was young in the image, barely nineteen, and wore the flowing robes of her status as princess of Alderaan. Her mouth moved to words that Luke could never forget. *Obi-Wan Kenobi, you're our only hope.*

Her words—and her beauty—had motivated his younger self to find the crazy old wizard in the deserts of Tatooine. As a consequence, that quest had saved him from the Imperial stormtroopers who burned his uncle and aunt to the bone.

Luke frowned at R2-D2. The astromech knew him too well. He was trying to make Luke feel guilty for abandoning his friends. "That's a cheap move."

Cheap though it might be, it was working. For as Leia's image flickered before him, Luke remembered he was more than the last of the Jedi.

He was also a brother.

Finn lay on a repulsorlift cart, being pulled in fits and starts down the corridor. He tried to kick, but nothing happened. His leg wouldn't respond and his wrists were in binders. "I . . . can't move . . ." he said. "You . . . stunned me. . . . *Help!*"

Rose glared down at him. "I'm taking you to the brig and turning you in for desertion."

"No!" he said. She had it all wrong. He had to make her understand he wasn't a deserter. He was just trying to warn Rey. "This fleet is doomed. If my friend comes back to it, she's doomed, too."

Rose let go of the cart and crouched down to his level. "You're a selfish traitor."

"Look," Finn said, his tongue able to move more freely now, "if I could save Rey by saving the Resistance fleet, I would, but I can't. Nobody can. We can't outrun the First Order fleet."

"We can jump to lightspeed," she said.

"They can track us through lightspeed."

Her suspicion turned into alarm. "They can track us through lightspeed?"

"Yes! They'll just show up seconds later and we'd have blown a ton of fuel, which we're dangerously short on." Finn started to wiggle his limbs. His paralysis was wearing off, but his jaw remained numb. "I can't feel my teeth. What did you shoot me with?"

Rose ignored his question, lost in thought. "Active tracking," she said. "Hyperspace tracking is new tech, but the principle must be the same as any active tracker. I've done maintenance on active trackers. They're single source, to avoid interference. So—"

Finn got the gist of what she was saying. If the First Order could operate only a single hyperspace tracker at a time, it would be installed on the most powerful vessel in the armada, the Mega-Destroyer.

"They're only tracking us from the lead ship!" they said at the same time.

He held up his bound wrists and gave her a beggar's smile. For a tense moment her suspicion seemed to return, but then she keyed the code and unlocked the binders.

Immediately the pair went to work hatching a plan. Rose believed she could shut the tracker down if she could gain access to the power breaker room on the Mega-Destroyer. Finn could lead her there. He knew the layout of the *Supremacy* by heart, having spent an entire training cycle with his trooper team mopping its floors. But they'd need a ship to transport them to the Mega-Destroyer. Since Rose was only a maintenance tech, she couldn't fly a Resistance shuttle for her own use.

Poe, however, would be able to get one for them.

They found the pilot in General Organa's quarters, by her bedside with C-3PO and BB-8. The general lay in a coma as medical droids fussed about her, caring for her every need.

Finn introduced Poe to Rose and pitched him their plan to sneak aboard the *Supremacy* and disable the tracker.

Even a temporary pause in the tracker's operation would give the Resistance enough time to jump to lightspeed without being followed.

BB-8 beeped his approval, but Poe was less persuaded. "Poe," Finn pleaded, "this'll save the fleet and save Rey. We have to do it."

Poe went over to General Organa on her bunk. He looked at her, touching her hand, as if to discern what she would advise.

"If I must be the sole voice of reason," interjected C-3PO, "Vice Admiral Holdo will never approve of this plan."

Poe's attitude suddenly changed. "You're right, Threepio. This plan is need-to-know. And *she* doesn't."

"Oh dear," said the protocol droid.

Poe looked at Finn and Rose. "So. How do we sneak you onto a Star Destroyer?"

"We steal a First Order shuttle," Rose suggested.

"No good," Poe said. "We need clearance codes."

"So we steal clearance codes," Rose said.

Finn shook his head. "They're bio-hexacrypt and rescrambled every hour. It's impossible. Their security shields are airtight. We can't get through them undetected. Nobody can."

"I'm sure somebody can, if there's money to be made," Poe said. "Threepio, reach out to your droid contacts on Takodana and see if you can get ahold of Maz Kanata."

The droid scolded Poe that he shouldn't be unmasking a top-secret spy network among present low-ranking company, but complied with the request. Not long after, the three-dimensional form of the tiny smuggler with big goggles appeared on the room's holotransceiver. Armed with a blaster, Maz appeared to be engaged in a firefight, shooting at unseen enemies.

Poe cut to the chase and asked her if she could get them clearance codes.

"Of course I could do it," Maz said, "but I'm a little tied down right now. Union dispute—you don't want to hear about it. But lucky for you there's exactly one guy I trust who can get you past that kind of security. A 'Master Codebreaker.' A soldier, freedom fighter, an ace pilot, a poet with a blaster, and the second-best smuggler I've ever met."

"Oh!" C-3PO exclaimed. "It sounds like this fellow can do everything."

"Oh, yes, he can." The way Maz said it, grinning and blinking her large eyes, reminded Finn of how she had flirted with Chewbacca when Han had taken them all to Takodana. It made Finn uncomfortable, and apparently Rose, too, from the grimace on her face.

A blaster bolt zinged past Maz. "And he's sympathetic to the Resistance," she added. "You'll find him at a high stakes table in the casino in Canto Bight."

"Canto Bight? But that's—" Poe stopped himself from elaborating further. "Maz, is there any way we can do this ourselves?"

Maz fired back at her foes. "Sorry, kiddo. You want on that Destroyer, you got one option: find the Master

Codebreaker. You'll know who he is by the red plom bloom he wears on his lapel—"

"Red plom what?" Finn asked. But the transmission cut out.

Their mission settled, Finn reluctantly gave Poe the wrist beacon for safekeeping. He realized that rather than seeking Rey out, the best thing he could do to save her life—to save *all* their lives—was disable that tracker so the Resistance could escape the Destroyers. Then Rey could follow the beacon back to the cruiser, without the threat of being killed or captured.

At least that was what Finn hoped.

The sun had not yet risen on Ahch-To when Luke returned to the village. But he did not go into his hut. He walked to the bench where Rey slept and waited. When her eyes opened, he spoke.

"Tomorrow. At dawn. Three lessons. I will teach you the ways of the Jedi—and why they need to end. And when you understand, you will leave me alone on this island to die."

He turned away from her and entered his hut, closing the door. Now it was time for him to rest so he could maintain the strength not to change his mind any more than he already had.

CHAPTER
10

STAY *here. I'll come back for you, sweetheart. I promise.*

The star freighter's hatch closed, and its engines warmed. Rey tried to run toward it, but Unkar Plutt's meaty hand held her back. No amount of squirming or wriggling would release her. She was only a small human child, while Plutt was an overweight, overgrown Crolute.

"Come back!" Rey shrieked at the ship. "Come back!"

Her cries caused Plutt to squeeze her arm so tightly it hurt. But that pain did not compare with the heartbreak of watching the freighter lift off. The ship roared toward Jakku's sun, never to come back as promised.

Rey woke to the sunlight of another world. Dawn streamed through the doorway of the hut in which she'd taken shelter to escape the night's rain. Fortunately, the rain had ended, as had the nightmare of her parents abandoning her on Jakku.

She blinked and the afterimages of the bad dream faded away. This day was too important to let them disturb her. She had to have all her focus if she was going to learn the ways of the Jedi.

Stretching her body, she slid off the stone bench and stepped toward the door, then stopped. She wasn't alone in the hut.

The presence of someone she knew lurked in the shadows. A brooding, angry presence. Kylo Ren.

She saw him, somehow, undergoing surgery. He winced as a droid pulled stitches from his face. She had cut him there during their fight and she could feel the ache and sting of the wound, as if Ren had drawn her into his suffering. His pupils burned with hate.

Instinctively, she drew the blaster Han Solo had given her and shot at the shadows.

The energy bolt drilled a hole through the wall. Light poured inside, dispelling the darkness. Kylo Ren was nowhere in sight.

Rey ran outside. To her relief, Kylo Ren didn't appear to be anywhere in the village, either. He'd just been another weird manifestation of this weird island. A ghost.

Or maybe not, as he materialized before her again. This time she could clearly see his mane of hair, his scarred face, his dark eyes. He gestured at her and said, "You will bring Luke Skywalker to me."

She almost laughed. Did this murderer think she would obey him? Did he think he could control her movements or extract her secrets as he had before? She would rather die than let him do those things to her again.

Ren dropped his hand, as if surprised by the power of

her rebuke. "You're not doing this . . . no. The effort would kill you." His eyes probed around her, only to settle back on her. "Can you see my surroundings?"

"You're going to pay for what you did," she said.

"I can't see yours," he said, ignoring her threat. "Just you. So no—this is something else."

Something else? What was he talking about? What was happening anyway? Was this even real?

Footsteps sounded behind her. She turned. Luke Skywalker stood outside his hut. She kept quiet out of fear. If Kylo Ren discovered she had found the Jedi Master, he could ruin the progress she had made.

Her silence, however, could not conceal her emotions from Ren. He snarled. "Luke . . ."

Luke stopped, peering past Rey. "What's that about?"

Rey spun back around toward Ren. But as before, her bitter enemy was not there. In Kylo Ren's place was a group of hairless humanoids in white robes and headdresses. Their skin was rubbery, like that of an amphibian, and tinted the gray-blue of the surrounding sea. Two large eyes rested on either side of their melon-shaped heads, with twin blow-holes and a pursed mouth between. They trundled about the village on three-toed feet, regarding Rey with distrust and mumbling to each other in a singsong tongue. One jabbed a fat finger at the hole Rey had blown in the wall of her hut.

Rey turned red, realizing Luke had been asking her

about the damage and not Kylo Ren. "I was cleaning my blaster, and . . . it went off."

Luke accepted her lie without further question. Another of the beings piped something at Luke, eyeing Rey. Luke responded in their language, then headed out of the village.

Eager to be away from Kylo Ren and those creatures, Rey followed Luke. He led her up another staircase, this one spiraling up the highest of the two mountains on the island.

"Who were those things?" she asked.

"Caretakers," Luke said. "Island natives. They've kept up the Jedi structures since they were built."

Rey glanced down at the village. The strange Caretaker beings were watching her. "I don't think they like me."

"Can't imagine what gave you that idea."

A section of the staircase hugged the cliff. Cooing and chirping sounded from small dark holes in the rock wall. The occasional avian perched on a step, blinking at Rey with big black eyes. "While you're being chatty, can you tell me what those chubby birdlike things are?" she asked.

"Porgs."

"*Porgs*?"

"Porgs," Luke said, without further comment.

After strenuous effort, they climbed the last stair and arrived on a short shelf of rock near the summit. A cave was carved into the mountain behind them. Rey felt a pull toward the mouth of the cave, as she had at the tree. Luke took her to the ledge instead.

The height provided an unsurpassed view of the ocean.

Giant waves crashed on rocks below, and the sky met the sea along a gray horizon. The sight should have relaxed her, but her conversation with Kylo Ren hung over her like a noxious cloud.

Luke broke a stalk off a plant that grew between the cracks in the rock. He rolled it back and forth in his palm. "What do you know about the Force?"

The truth was she knew virtually nothing. On Jakku, no one talked about the Force. Life was too hard to believe in anything that didn't immediately put food in your belly. But she dared not show Luke her ignorance.

"It's a power that the Jedi have, that lets them control people and . . . make things float," she said, fumbling through what little she knew.

"Impressive," Luke quipped. "Every word in that sentence was wrong."

Rey felt foolish for not asking Leia more. She had left D'Qar in such a rush, with barely enough time to say goodbye to Finn.

Luke gestured to a large smooth rock. "Lesson one. Sit here. Legs crossed."

When she had seated herself atop the stone, Luke spoke with a reverence she had not heard from him before. "The Force is not a power you have. It's not about floating rocks. It's the energy between all things, a tension, a balance that binds the universe together."

"Okay," Rey said. His description could've characterized a thousand other mystical traditions. "But what *is* it?"

"Close your eyes."

Annoyed he wouldn't give her an answer, she still did as he said. Her world soon became one of sound—waves breaking, gulls cawing, and the measured tones of Luke's voice.

"Breathe," he said.

She exhaled and inhaled, filling her lungs with the salty sea air. With every breath, her heartbeat slowed and her impatience receded. A calmness she had never experienced on Jakku settled over her.

"Now . . . reach out."

She lifted an arm and stretched out her hand. Something danced on the tips of her fingers. "I feel something."

"You feel it?"

Most definitely, she did—so much that it tickled. "Yes, I feel it!"

"That's the Force," Luke said.

"Really?" It seemed so easy to access its power. Just a few breaths and her palm tingled with new energy. If she had only known this method before, her hardscrabble life could've been far different.

Luke sounded equally astounded. "It must be really strong with you."

Her confidence soared. That was the first nice thing he had said about her. "Well, I—"

She yelped as pain shot through her palm. Opening her eyes, she realized that what she had felt wasn't the Force at all, but a reed Luke held. He had smacked her hand with it.

Her cheeks reddened in embarrassment at being so

easily tricked. Luke hadn't been talking about stretching out her hands at all. "You meant reach out like . . ." Not knowing exactly how to define it, she pointed to her center—her heart. He nodded.

"Okay, got it." She shut her eyes, determined to try again.

Luke moved her arms so her palms touched the stone on which she sat. It helped her resist the temptation to use her limbs.

"Breathe," Luke said once more. "Just breathe."

Out and in went her breaths, slowly but surely. With them went her confusion and her questions. Peace returned, deeper than before.

"Now," Luke said, "reach out with your feelings."

Rey didn't think about what he had said. She just let it happen. Every one of her senses reached out, rather than one dominating the others. A new awareness of the world came to her, informed by the little things she would have missed otherwise. She felt moisture on the boulder beneath her. Smelled the algae that flourished in the seashore pools. Tasted a gust of moldy air coming from within the cave. Heard the mating song of some faraway leviathan.

"What do you see?" Luke asked.

Though her eyes were closed, images flashed in her mind. "The island," she told him, perceiving it in all its glory, as if she were one of the gulls gliding above. It was quickly replaced by a vision of flowers blooming before her. "Life," she said, enjoying the flowers' lovely fragrance, yet also sniffing out the rot in the soil from which they grew. "Death and decay," she added, watching blades of grass shoot from the dirt, "that feeds new life."

A view of the mountainside presented itself, splendid in the sunlight. "Warmth," Rey said, shuddering as she was plunged deep into the sea, "and coldness."

Her perception returned to the cliff, where a mother porg doted over her nest. "Peace," Rey observed, touched by the maternal affection. But as before, the scene was swiftly upended. A wave smashed into the nest. "Violence," she said, as the sea snatched the eggs.

"And between it all?" Luke asked.

Rey shifted her attention. She let the images and smells, feelings and sounds fade into the background and instead concentrated on the ways those details came to her, the paths that brought her senses alive.

Luke was right. There was something in between. It connected her to the rock, the porgs, the sea, the waves, the island. It was untouchable yet tangible, invisible yet bright. "A balance," she described, "of energy."

Yet it was more than a source of power. Much more. A set of principles governed it. It held influence, yet did not judge. Most simply, it attracted things—like gravity, like love.

"A . . . force," she said.

"And inside you?"

"Inside me . . ." And there it was, encompassing her, too, as if there were no difference between the inside and the out. "That same force."

"This is the lesson," Luke said. "The Force does not

belong to the Jedi. It is so much bigger. To say that if the Jedi die, the light dies is vanity."

The joy of discovery was short-lived. Her senses took control. "There's something else here. A powerful light. Blinding."

"This is the first Jedi temple. The concentration of light."

"But there's something else." In her mind's eye she saw a hole in the rock, ringed by a reddish moss. "Beneath the island. A place. A dark place. It's cold. It's calling me."

Luke's voice took on a new urgency. "Resist it, Rey. Fight it!"

She couldn't. The darkness swallowed her up. She heard a roar. Felt a shake. The ground moved. A chorus of stars shrilled in the skies. A fountain gushed from the underground cove. Someone called her name. Luke? Where was he? Should he not be here, too? In the Force? It was supposed to connect everything and everyone.

"Rey—Rey!"

Her vision ended in pain. Luke smacked her awake. She choked on air and shivered. She was wet, as if she had actually gone underwater. "That place," she said, remembering to breathe, "was trying to—"

Luke didn't let her explain. "You went straight to the dark. It offered you something you needed and you didn't even try to stop yourself."

He started toward the cave behind them. Rey staggered up from the rock. "I saw everything—the island, and past it . . . I felt the stars singing. I thought my heart would explode, but . . . I didn't see you. Nothing from you, no light, no dark."

Even here, as she stood before him, she couldn't sense him. Why? Wasn't he a Jedi Master? Shouldn't he shine brighter than anything else?

"You've closed yourself off from the Force," Rey said. Luke wasn't merely hiding out from the rest of the galaxy. He was hiding from the very thing that had made his destiny.

Her accusation fell on deaf ears. "I've seen this raw strength only once before—in Ben Solo," Luke said. "It didn't scare me enough then. It does now."

Luke entered the cave. Rey remained on the ledge, still in shock. She noticed cracks in the dirt surrounding her. A chunk of the mountainside had collapsed into the sea. When had that happened? Had she somehow caused a landslide?

She looked into the mouth of the cave, then turned away.

CHAPTER
11

WITH Poe's help, Finn and Rose commandeered a transport pod and flew away from the *Raddus*, unnoticed by Vice Admiral Holdo. The pod's small size made it indiscernible to the First Order's active tracker, allowing it to leap into hyperspace without attracting any pursuit. It arrived in the Cantonica system exactly according to plan, but for one small issue. Finn found a stowaway next to the toilet.

"Beebee-Ate! What are you doing here?"

The droid rolled out of the restroom into the main cabin, beeping innocently.

Lingering at the door, Rose raised an eyebrow at the droid. "Watching after us?" She looked at Finn. "We're on approach. Strap in."

Finn glared at the droid. "How do you say 'Poe's going to kill me' in beep?" BB-8 should have been assisting Poe on the *Raddus*, not trying to supervise them like some pint-sized babysitter.

The droid sniped back something Finn knew was best left untranslated.

Finn followed Rose into the cockpit. The orb of Cantonica hung before them out the viewport. A medium-sized ocean added a splash of blue to the otherwise drab and desert-covered planet. Along the ocean's crescent edge lay their intended destination, the blinking lights of Canto Bight.

"It's a terrible place filled with the worst people in the galaxy," Rose informed Finn. She didn't justify how she knew this and spent the rest of the descent trying to teach Finn the technique of landing a transport pod. The result was more of a crash than a landing. Luckily, Finn had touched down on a beach and the sand absorbed much of the impact.

When they disembarked, an Abednedo in a white robe started jabbering at them that they'd landed on a public beach. They ignored him and hurried along the boardwalk into the city.

Finn saw that Rose was wrong about Cantonica's capital. The city didn't seem terrible to him at all. In fact, it was one of the most astounding places he'd ever visited.

Sailboats and yachts drifted in the bay, glowing in the sunset. Luxury landspeeders cruised the coastal highways. Shoreline hotels offered romantic retreats for the wealthy and the connected. For those who couldn't afford an ocean view, such fortune might be won a block away. The main strip of Canto Bight's renowned casinos glittered like a case of gems, with each establishment trying to outshine the others in extravagance.

Maz had not divulged where exactly the Master Codebreaker could be found, so they entered the largest gambling den they came across, the Canto Casino. It was a palace for high-stakes gambling, where millions of credits were bet on everything from jubilee wheels and zinbiddle tournaments to pongobungo cards and even blob races. Musicians tootled current hits from a side stage, waiters and waitresses walked the floor serving free drinks, and all the patrons were dressed in the height of fashion. Finn was exhilarated. "This place is great!"

Rose shared none of his enthusiasm. "Maz said this Master Codebreaker would have a red plom bloom on his lapel. Let's find him and get out of here."

Finn started after her, noticing that BB-8 was waylaid behind them. A monocled amphibian in white tie and tails, burping from the booze he was drinking, mistook the ball droid for a lugjack machine and jammed credit chips into BB-8's data slot.

Finn wasn't worried. BB-8 would catch up with them. The astromech had handled worse than an intoxicated gambler.

Rose maintained a brisk pace through the busy casino, glancing at people's lapels. Finn spent more time eyeing the people themselves. Though his knowledge of popular culture was minimal, even he recognized that some of these beings were the galaxy's rich and famous.

A loud braying sound disrupted Finn's people-watching, and the heart-pounding rumble that succeeded it caused both him and Rose to shrink back. A pack of long-eared, long-limbed creatures galloped past the window wall to the glee of the patrons.

Rose's eyes widened. "Were those what I think they were?" Without explanation, she hurried under an arch, leaving the casino floor.

Finn joined her on an outdoor balcony. Below them graceful four-legged beasts raced around a circular track, spurred by jockeys on their backs and spectators in the stands. "What are those things?"

Rose gawked at the creatures. "Fathiers. They were my sister's favorite animals when we were kids. She never got to see one. So beautiful."

Finn peered through a pair of electrobinoculars mounted to the balcony's rail. The enhanced view showed him just how majestic the fathiers were. They held their tawny heads high and raced with a noble pride, even as their jockeys spurred them with electro-whips.

If she could admire the beauty in these beasts, Finn wondered why she couldn't see it around her in Canto Bight. "This whole place is beautiful. Why do you hate it so much?" he asked.

Rose scowled. "My sister and I grew up in a poor mining system. The First Order stripped our ore to finance their military, then shelled us to test their weapons. They took everything we had." Rose swept her gaze across the well-dressed spectators. "And who do you think these people are? Only one business in the galaxy gets you this rich."

"War," Finn said grimly.

Rose nodded. "Selling weapons to the First Order, getting rich off of so much suffering. Back home . . ." She clutched her necklace's medallion. "I wish I could put my fist through this whole lousy, beautiful town."

BB-8 darted up to them, making a racket with the credit chips clattering inside his round body. He parked before Rose and let out a rapid series of beeps.

"Red plom bloom?" Rose started looking around. "Where?—*ow!*"

Finn jabbed her, indicating a stylish human with slicked-back hair at one of the high-stakes gaming tables. A crimson-petaled flower was pinned to the lapel of a white dinner jacket.

"The Master Codebreaker," Rose whispered.

Finn immediately understood how Maz could be so smitten by the man. He was the swankiest of all the swanky gamblers in the casino, with the aura of a magnetic charge. Admirers, particularly female, cozied up to him, blushing whenever he winked at them. He oozed confidence like a Hutt in heat, and even with untold credits on the table, he juggled dice as if the act of rolling them were a mere formality and his fortune guaranteed.

The Abednedo from the beach cut in front of them. "These are the guys," he said.

A high-voltage zap in Finn's back stopped him from asking questions. He quickly found himself being arrested by the Canto Bight police.

As he was cuffed, Finn caught an offhand glance from the Master Codebreaker. But then the man turned away and cast his dice to the cheers of his audience.

CHAPTER
12

FROM the window of his ready room, Kylo Ren observed the flurry of activity down in the *Supremacy*'s hangar. Stormtrooper platoons boarded assault shuttles. Pilots strapped themselves into TIE fighters. Support staff maglocked droid walkers to the sides of transports. In the center stood Captain Phasma, her chrome armor spotless, her red-trimmed cape hanging from a shoulder.

Rumors abounded that saboteurs had waylaid Phasma on Starkiller Base and thrown her into a trash compactor. Even if there was truth to the rumor, a trash compactor would have never ended the career of a soldier of her stature. Though she usually sided with General Hux, Ren was pleased she hadn't met her demise. Phasma would lead the First Order's forces in eradicating the Resistance wherever it dared to make its last stand. Victory would soon be at hand.

But there was another adversary that needed to be vanquished. The scavenger. The girl. Rey.

He felt the tingle of her presence again, like cobwebs that couldn't be swept from his mind. How they were connected to each other, he didn't know. The girl did not seem powerful enough to communicate this way. But linked they were, and it was of no consequence that Rey might be halfway across the galaxy. The Force was not bound by the limitations of space, distance, or time.

He sensed her standing in the rain, near the dilapidated junk heap of a ship Han Solo had once owned. His nostrils flared in disgust.

When Ren's mind intruded on hers, she was thinking of someone else: the renegade stormtrooper who had betrayed the First Order and attacked Ren on Starkiller Base. FN-2187. The one she called Finn.

She was concerned about him—so much so that she'd just had her barbaric Wookiee friend send a message to the Resistance and was contemplating sending another. Ren laughed. It was he who had delivered the blow that had gravely wounded Finn. He hoped the traitor died.

Discerning Ren's presence, the girl hissed, "Murderous snake."

Her recognition solidified their bond. She could see him and Ren could see her, as if they existed in the same place. He went toward her. Rain ran down her face.

"You're late," she said. "You lost. I found Skywalker."

"And how's that going?" Ren asked with a chuckle. "Has he told you what happened? The night I destroyed his temple? Has he told you why?"

"I know everything I need to know about you."

"You do?" Ren mused. "Yes, you do . . . You have that

look in your eyes from our little forest duel, when you called me a monster."

Rey stood firm. "You are a monster."

"Yes," he said. "I am."

Ren broke the connection, opening his eyes. He was alone again, in the ready room. But his affirmation about himself lingered in his mind.

A monster. Indeed that was what he had become.

Beads of moisture tingled his scar. He wiped his face and noticed his glove was also dripping wet, as if he had been outside with Rey. He clenched his fist, wringing out the rain.

To shake off the contact with Kylo Ren, Rey worked up a sweat and practiced with her staff as she often had on Jakku. She targeted a large, jagged standing stone with each end, ducking, parrying, and jumping, as if she faced a real opponent—as if she faced Kylo Ren.

After a bout of exercise, she paused for a brief rest. Her eyes fell on her satchel, which lay on the ground where she had dropped it. The hilt of Luke's lightsaber protruded from its pocket.

She glanced at the boulder, then back at her hilt. It occurred to her that if she wanted to master the Jedi path, she would also have to master the lightsaber. She could not rely on pure adrenaline alone to defeat more skilled opponents like Kylo Ren.

Rey put down her staff and picked up the hilt. Flicking the activation button, she extended the blade and marveled at its bright blue beam, nearly weightless in her hand. This lightsaber had played a large role in recent galactic history, and here she was holding it as if it were her own.

Wielding the saber, she resumed her duel against the standing stone, slashing and blocking an invisible foe's blade, careful not to strike the rock itself. As Luke had taught her, she focused on her breath and opened all her senses. In nudges and tugs, she began to feel the Force guiding her movements, as if she were a dancer swaying to music.

"Impressive."

Luke's voice jarred her back to the here and now. Her blade sizzled through the air to bite into stone, cleaving the boulder in two. Its upper chunk fell away and tumbled down the mountainside to smash into a wheeled cart at the bottom. The pair of Caretakers who had been pulling the cart glared up at her.

Rey cringed, switching off the lightsaber. She hadn't meant to do that.

Luke stood behind her. She had the feeling he'd been watching her for a while. He beckoned her to follow him.

They climbed up the mountain stairs, returning to the meditation ledge. But this time he did not give breathing lessons or riddles. He led her through the mouth of the cave that had pulled at her before and into the Jedi temple.

The entrance widened into a spacious chamber. Rey

followed Luke to a pool in the middle, circled by a retaining wall. "I've shown that you don't need the Jedi to use the Force," Luke said. "So why do you need the Jedi Order?"

Rey didn't overthink her reply. "To fight the rising darkness. They kept the peace for a thousand generations." Her reflection stared back at her in the glassy pool, while Luke's held a frown. "And I can tell from your look that every word I just said was wrong."

Luke's tone turned grim. "Lesson two. Now that they're extinct, the Jedi are romanticized, deified like gods. But if you strip away the myth and look at their deeds, the legacy of the Jedi is failure, hypocrisy, hubris."

"That's not true," Rey protested. On Jakku, she had studied the old tales, even paid hefty portions of food to traders to hear any story of the Jedi they knew. Some of the Jedi might have been liars and hypocrites, but they could not be deemed failures if they had protected the galaxy for as long as they had.

Luke grew more somber as he spoke. "At the height of their powers, the Jedi allowed Darth Sidious to rise, create the Empire, and wipe them out. It was a Jedi Master who was responsible for the training and creation of Darth Vader."

"And a Jedi who saved him," Rey countered. In her opinion, Luke seemed to be a little hard on the Jedi and himself. According to the tales, his training in the Jedi way had enabled him defeat the Emperor and pull Darth Vader away from the dark side before his death. "Vader may have been the most hated man in the galaxy, but you saw there was conflict inside him. You believed that he wasn't gone, he could be turned."

"And I became a legend," Luke said with a sigh. "For many years there was balance. I took no Padawans and no darkness rose. But then I saw Kylo"—he hesitated before correcting himself—"Ben, my nephew, with the mighty Skywalker blood. In my hubris I thought I could train him, I could pass on my strength. I might not be the last Jedi."

His gaze shifted away from the pool. "Han," he said, "Han was . . . Han about it. He would've preferred his son learn to use a blaster rather than a lightsaber. But Leia trusted me with her son. I took him, and a dozen students, and began a training temple. By the time I realized I was no match for the darkness rising in him, it was too late."

"What happened?" Rey asked. This part of the tales she didn't know. No one did.

Luke looked into the cavern's shadows. Some moments passed before he spoke. "One night I came to him in his sleeping quarters, to see if I could resolve the matter." His voice strained. "He woke and saw me standing there, and then . . . the darkness exploded within him. He called on the Force to bring down the ceiling on me. I was incapacitated and it was a long time before I dragged myself out of the rubble. He must've thought I was dead."

Luke turned back to the pool. Its waters were still and clear. "When I came to, the temple was burning. Kylo left with a handful of my students and slaughtered the rest."

His story triggered Rey's memory. She recalled the vision she'd had on Takodana of Luke, cowled in a black cloak, kneeling and touching R2-D2 with his artificial hand. A structure burned in the background. It must have been the temple that Luke had built.

Luke let out a heavy breath. "Leia blamed Snoke. But it was me. I failed."

Rey could feel the anguish of his soul, mired in self-doubt. "You didn't fail Kylo. He failed you." She fixed her gaze on Luke. "I won't."

The wind whistled through the cave mouth. But as she listened, she heard, she *felt*, there was something more to the sound than a subtle change of the breeze. Had Kylo Ren found them so quickly?

She hastened out of the cave onto the ledge. Half a dozen wooden boats traversed the sea to the island. This wasn't the First Order. They would never ride in something so primitive.

Luke came to stand behind her. "It's a tribe from a neighboring island. They come once a month to raid and plunder the Caretakers' village."

Just as he described, the boats slewed toward the coast. Yet it gave Rey no relief they weren't allied to the First Order. She might not have endeared herself to the Caretakers, yet she didn't wish them harm.

"We've got to stop them," she said. "Come on!"

Luke didn't move a muscle. "Do you know what a true Jedi Knight would do right now?" He paused, as if to impart weight to his answer. "Nothing."

His indifference shocked her. This was not the time for lessons. It was time for action. The speeders were landing as they spoke. "They're gonna get hurt. We have to help!"

"If you meet the raiding party with force, they'll be back next month with greater numbers and greater violence. Will you be here next month?"

How did that matter? She was here now, and she could do something. She wasn't going to stand idly by. It infuriated her that he—a Jedi Master—would even suggest it.

"That burn inside you, that anger thinking of what the raiders are going to do," Luke said, "the books in the Jedi library say ignore that. Only act when you can maintain balance. Even if people get hurt."

It was one of the stupidest things Rey had ever heard. If that was Jedi wisdom, she wanted nothing to do with it.

She hopped off the ledge and slid down the mountainside.

"Wait—Rey!" Luke called.

Somehow, she kept her footing on the steep path, zigzagging down the cliff until she got to the bottom. The village lay just beyond the tidal pools. Shrieks and screams echoed from the common area.

Rey pulled the lightsaber from her satchel, switched on the blade, and ran as fast as she could, splashing through the shallow pools. Arriving in the village, she rushed into a crowd of Caretakers and let out a battle cry, holding the lightsaber high.

The shrieking momentarily stopped. Large eyes blinked at her. Rey took a few steps back. The raiders were males of the same species as the Caretakers. Yet instead of plundering and pillaging, they were dancing and drinking with their female counterparts.

Luke had lied to her. This wasn't a raid. She had barged into a matchmaking celebration.

The males and females welcomed her with hoots and hurrahs. High-pitched notes were played on makeshift instruments. Youths waved clumps of glowing seaweed. Chewbacca and R2-D2 even barked and beeped at her, whooping it up with some Caretakers in the back.

Doing her best to hide her embarrassment, Rey waved her lightsaber back at them as if in greeting. Everyone went wild.

The party resumed full force, though Rey didn't partake in the festivities for long. She managed to slip away, finding refuge on the porch of a hut. Here she stared out at the sea as the moon rose, stewing in anger. How could Luke have done that to her? Was she nothing but a fool to him? Had he no care for anything other than himself?

A faint light shone through the lip of her satchel. She opened the bag and took out the beacon bracelet she'd tucked away for safe keeping. Its glow would have been imperceptible in the sunlight, but in the darkness, it shed a soft incandescence that reassured her. Leia had said if the beacon went dark, it signaled that Rey should not come back. The light's persistence suggested that the Resistance also persisted.

Rey thought of Leia, who in a mere couple of days on

D'Qar had shown Rey what a good mother and a strong woman could be. And then she thought of Finn, the one true friend she'd met in a long time. Had he recovered from his wounds? Might he be thinking of her?

She felt selfish abandoning him to journey to Ahch-To when he had risked his life to save her on Starkiller Base. If something happened to him while she was away, she'd never forgive herself.

She placed the beacon back in her satchel, hearing someone approach. She knew who it was, and her anger at him for tricking her returned. "'Raid and plunder'?" she asked.

"In a way," Luke said.

"I thought they were in danger. I was trying to do something!"

"Then ask what the Resistance truly needs. Because it's not an old, failed husk of a religion."

She turned to him, this sad man in filthy robes. "The legend of Luke Skywalker that you hate so much. I believed in it," she said. "I was wrong."

It hurt to say those words, because they denied her past and her dreams. But as of now, they were the truth.

She walked off, not looking back until Luke was but a shade in the moonlight.

CHAPTER
13

ROSE grabbed the bars of the jail cell where the Canto Bight police had unceremoniously dumped her and Finn. "This is a big mistake. We didn't do anything!"

The man standing guard rolled his eyes. "You crashed a shuttle on a public beach."

It peeved her he had called it a crash. Sure, she could've down better in teaching Finn how to land the craft, and they might have dug up a hole, but the transport pod had remained intact. "What, did we break the sand? You can't break sand! Hey, don't—"

The guard went down the corridor, leaving them alone. She withdrew from the bars and paced. Finn, meanwhile, tried his luck on the cell door's lock. He pressed random keys on its code pad, shook the mechanism a couple of times, and prodded the hole with his fingernail.

"So after that totally works, what's our plan?" Rose asked.

The lock buzzed, and for a moment she thought maybe he'd actually done it, but then a metal plate dropped over the keypad. Finn gave up.

"The thing that failed was our plan," he said. "Without a thief to break us into that Destroyer, it's shot. And even if they let us out in the morning and find him, our fleet will be out of time. We're done."

A hoarse voice spoke up behind them. "Hey, I'm a thief."

The cell was big, and from one of its dark corners, a stranger rose from a squeaky bunk. He was middle-aged and human, though he might've also passed for one of the gigantic rats Rose had seen on the march to the jailhouse. He wore a shabby leather duster over raggedy clothes and scratched himself all over rather rudely. His boots were tied together by the laces, allowing him to hang them over his neck. "Sorry, couldn't help but overhear all the boring stuff you were saying really loudly while I was trying to sleep. Thief? Codebreaker?" He lifted two dirt-caked thumbs, indicating himself. "Yo."

"Yeah . . . we're not talking about picking pockets," Finn said.

Their cellmate chuckled to himself. "Don't let the wrapper fool you, friend. Me and First Order codeage go way back. If the price is right, I can break you into old man Snoke's b-boudoir."

"We're good," Rose said.

The man shrugged, as if it was their loss.

"Besides," Finn said, "if you're such a good thief, what are you doing in here?"

"Brother, this is the one place in town I can get some sleep without worrying about the cops." He took a cap from the bed and placed it on his head, giving it a rakish tilt. A rust-rimmed silver band was stitched into the cap's fabric, inscribed with the words DON'T JOIN in large letters. "Let me take a look at the lock."

Finn moved aside as the self-proclaimed thief shuffled over to the lock and tinkered with it. After a tap, the door opened.

He walked out, as if there were nothing to it.

Rose looked at Finn, astonished. Then sirens rang out. Hurrying through the door, they couldn't see where the thief had gone, so they turned and ran down the corridor.

Prisoners called out from the cells they dashed past. More alarms sounded. A voice crackled over a comm. "Lock down the exits! Everyone fan out!"

Glowrods shone ahead and behind, getting nearer every second. The guards were closing in on them.

Rose's boot clanged on something metallic. An iron grill was set in the floor. She and Finn managed to wrench it loose. A great stink wafted out of the hole, so awful she had to cover her nose and mouth. But they were out of options. Either they went down there or they got caught. And if they got caught, they'd be thrown somewhere far worse than the city sewer.

She seized the top rung of a ladder and hastened down into the gloom. Before descending behind her, Finn tried to drag the heavy grill back in place. It wouldn't move no matter how hard he heaved, so he left the hole uncovered and scrambled down the ladder.

At first they argued about what direction to take, until

echoes above them forced them to choose. Rather than follow the sewage down to its drainage point, they headed up the tunnel's slight slope. Finn had to stoop so he didn't bump his head.

"This brings back memories—foul memories," Finn said, splashing through the muck. "Spent a training cycle cleaning the waste system on Starkiller Base."

Rose did her best to breathe only through her mouth. "You mopped floors, cleaned sewers . . . I thought you were a stormtrooper?"

"That's how the First Order made us into troopers. Either you learn how to fight or you're scrubbing filth the rest of your short life."

The farther they went, the nastier the stench grew, and soon Rose felt she might pass out. She was on the verge of doing so when they finally came across another ladder. She shimmied up the rungs after Finn, delighted to leave the sewer—except that the next place they climbed into didn't smell any better.

They emerged in the racetrack stables, where magnificent fathiers were held in dingy stalls. One of the animals thrust its muzzle through the boards to sniff them. It still wore its saddle from the night's race.

Ignoring the stink, Rose stepped right up to it, wanting to pet it. She stopped when she saw a haggard, half-starved stable boy staring back at her. He dropped the broom he was using to clean the stall and reached for an alarm on the wall.

"No, no, no!" Finn shouted.

"We're with the Resistance!" Rose said. As proof of where her loyalties lay, she flicked the catch on her ring. It slid open to reveal the starbird insignia of the old Rebel Alliance.

The boy's hand dropped away from the alarm button. Slowly, he smiled and she smiled back. A commotion outside abbreviated a more formal introduction. The guards were on their tail.

The stable boy opened the pen and gave the fathier a slap on its rump. The beast lowered its hind legs to the ground. Rose mounted first, then Finn. Another tap on its rear and the fathier was up, quickening toward a pair of doors that opened to the racetrack.

"How'd you know the kid would help us?" Finn asked.

"On my home planet, there are too many like him, whose families the First Order destroyed. Most are secret supporters of the Resistance."

The barn doors opened ahead of them, right as they heard a loud crash behind them. The Canto Bight police breached the stable and rushed inside. "There they are!" yelled the captain.

Grinning at Rose, the boy keyed a panel. Every stall in the stable opened. The captive fathiers sprinted for their freedom, blocking the cops from Rose and Finn.

Rose and Finn's fathier shot out onto the racetrack. She held its neck, and Finn clutched her waist. The creature had accelerated so quickly that a fall off its back would result in a snapped neck, a broken spine, or being trampled by the herd following close behind.

Police speeders whooshed above them, lighting up the night sky. The speeders were designed to maneuver through the confines of a city, and their operators sat in harnesses rigged to a control board and four horizontal stabilizers that assisted in balance. Guns on the speeders' central vanes took aim.

But the fathier Rose and Finn rode was no simple-minded beast. Aware of the danger, it snuffed and bolted off the racetrack, through the window wall of the casino.

Rose covered her face as glass shattered around her. The fathier burst through the cocktail lounge, smashing into the bar and leading the herd in a stampede around the casino. Gaming tables were given the hoof. Jubilee wheels went flying off their spinners. Credits spewed out of toppled lugjack machines. The rich and famous fled for their lives.

Rose and Finn's fathier carried them through another window out to the front of the casino. Valets scattered as the herd went on a mad dash into the city center, toppling luxury landspeeders, café chairs, and anything else that stood in their way. The police resumed their chase from above, but their spotlights and repulsorjets couldn't keep up with the beasts.

The herd veered down an alley, then raced along the rooftops of a lower level of the city. Their hooves pulverized a sunroof and the entire herd dropped into a steamy sauna occupied by an assortment of species, some toweled, some not, all sweating. After a brief scramble, the fathiers righted themselves and surged out of the building, losing little momentum as they pounded the pavement of the streets.

Rose inhaled the wind. "Yee-haw!" This was even better than she'd ever imagined. Her sister would have loved it.

Finn, however, moaned in terror as their fathier made a beeline for the sea wall.

A breath before imminent collision, the lead fathier leapt over the wall and the herd followed suit. They landed on the beach and galloped along the moonlit ocean, kicking up sand.

Energy beams lanced out from the pursuing speeders. One struck a fathier. It skidded and fell, but the stampede didn't stop, going ever faster.

The beach terminated in a bluff. As with the wall, the herd ran toward it, but it was much too high to hurdle. Instead, their hooves bit into the ground and they clambered up the side of the bluff. Rose clutched the fathier's neck as tightly as she could while Finn nearly squeezed out all the breath in her lungs.

Coming to a ledge, the fathiers continued their run in single file, rounding the bluff. But the climb had slowed them, allowing the police speeders to catch up. One by one, fathiers tumbled off the cliff, hit by the speeders' weapons.

"This is a shooting gallery," Finn said. "Get us out!"

As she had seen heroines do in holofilms, Rose pulled the fathier's soft mane to turn it to the right. It obeyed, rushing up a steep and rocky path to emerge in a meadow with the herd behind it.

Grasslands were the fathiers' natural terrain, and on it the creatures quickly outdistanced the police. But Rose couldn't bear any more fathiers being mowed down for her benefit. She clicked her tongue and yanked the mane again, trusting that the jockeys on Cantonica used the same gestures as they did on Otomok.

They did. While the rest of the herd veered left, Rose and Finn's mount slewed to the right. As Rose had hoped, the spotlights of the police speeders stayed on them and not the other fathiers.

"They're letting the herd go!" Rose shouted. "Now if we can just—"

Finn screamed at the top of his lungs. *"Cliff!"*

The fathier halted in a spray of dirt, casting them off. Rose thumped into the ground, saved from broken bones by the cushy grass. When she and Finn got back on their feet, they found themselves standing on the edge of a vast ravine, the ocean swirling hundreds of meters below. The other edge—if there was one—was hidden in the darkness.

The police speeders neared, their headlamps getting brighter. "Well, it was worth it to tear up that town," Finn said. "Make 'em hurt."

Rose knew Finn was just trying to put a good face on a terrible situation, but right then her only concern was for the fathier that had taken them here.

She unharnessed the saddle from its back. "Thank you." She gave the loyal beast a gentle smack and it galloped off to rejoin its herd. "Now it's worth it."

Something loud whirred behind them. Rose turned, about to raise her hands in surrender, and saw the ship that rose from the ravine. It was a trim star yacht, sporting twin speedvanes on the prow, the kind of craft one only saw in racing mags, a rich person's dream. It could only be owned by—

"The Master Codebreaker?" A hatch popped open on its hull and an astromech dome peeped out.

"Beebee-Ate!" Finn said. "Are you flying that thing?"

The droid assailed them in binary for leaving him behind in the casino. "No, we were coming back for you," Finn said, eyeing the approaching speeders. "Just come on, pick us up!"

Their former cellmate with the cap came up behind BB-8. "Oh, you need a lift? Say the magic words."

"Pretty . . . please?" Finn stammered.

The thief scowled. Rose knew that manners weren't what moved men like this.

"You're hired," she said.

Those were the magic words. The man lowered the ramp and they boarded. Before the hatch fully closed, the yacht had rocketed past the cops to an altitude airspeeders couldn't reach—the stars.

CHAPTER
14

"**CHEWIE,** get her ready for launch. We're leaving."

Rey spoke into her comlink as she backtracked along the same path that had taken her to Luke the day of her arrival. Now it would return her to the *Millennium Falcon* and the Resistance. She was done trying to persuade the stubborn Skywalker. He was a lost cause.

A dark presence pinched the back of her mind, as it had twice before. She gritted her teeth. "I'd rather not do this now."

"Me too," Kylo Ren said.

She spun around at the sound of his voice. "Why did you hate your father?"

"Because he was a weak-minded fool," Ren snarled. She saw him standing in his lair on a Star Destroyer, shirtless, his torso as pale as bleached bone.

Rey momentarily looked away in embarrassment, even though the vision came to her through the Force. "Give me an honest answer. You had a father who loved you."

"I didn't hate him."

His lie incensed her. "Then why did you kill him? I don't understand."

"No?" Ren said with a laugh. "Your own parents threw you away like garbage—"

"No, they didn't," Rey objected.

"Oh, they did, and you still can't stop needing them. It's your greatest weakness. You look for them everywhere. In Han Solo, and now in Skywalker."

Rey wanted to protest, but she had nothing to say. For once, Kylo Ren told the truth. After meeting Finn, Han Solo, and Chewbacca, she hadn't returned to Jakku to wait for her parents as she kept asserting she would. She'd stayed with Han because he'd taken her under his wing. Even after Kylo Ren had murdered him, she didn't go back. She went to Ahch-To, leaving friends like Finn behind, to find someone else to mentor her.

She was selfish, she realized—for what she sought was more than a mentor.

She wanted a parent.

Ren's lips curled into a smile. He turned the conversation back to Luke. "Did he tell you what happened that night?"

"Yes," she said. But she doubted Luke had told her every detail—and she knew Ren could sense her doubt.

"No he didn't," Ren said.

A new vision came to Rey, showing Kylo Ren's personal quarters in the Jedi temple. Ren slept on a pallet, visible in a crackling green glow.

Luke Skywalker, robed in black, hovered over him, holding his lightsaber. The Jedi Master's face was not the aged and tired one Rey knew, but a twisted and tormented face. The face of a monster.

Luke lowered his saber to kill the youth.

But Ren was already awake and called his own lightsaber to him. His blue blade parried Luke's green one. The swords sizzled. Energy sparked. Ren stretched out with his other hand to the ceiling. It quaked, fractured, and then caved in on Luke Skywalker.

"Liar," Rey said, cutting off the vision. Luke may not have told her all the truth, but he could never be a murderer.

Could he?

"Let the past die," Kylo Ren said. "Kill it if you have to. That's the only way to become what you were meant to be."

His image and presence disappeared from her mind. Yet his words remained, like salt in a wound.

She felt another nudge in the Force, down the cliff but in the opposite direction of the *Falcon*. She didn't resist the pull. She proceeded toward it. While she was still on this world, she was determined to learn all the secrets Luke wouldn't teach her.

She reached a large hole in the ground. Dark moss grew around the edge. It was the same hole she'd seen in her vision when training with Luke. A place of darkness.

She bent down and touched the moss. It was spongy and moist, yet offered no clues to what lay below. She looked around her. Little else thrived on this plane of rock.

Her foot slipped. She couldn't right her balance. The moss under her split and she fell, into the darkness, into the hole.

She landed with a splash in a pool of water. Gasping, she paddled to an outcropping of stone. She was lucky she didn't drown. Swimming lessons had not been a priority on Jakku.

She heaved herself onto the ledge, discovering she was in a cavern, probably beneath the ocean. And standing before her, dripping wet, her hair undone from the plunge, was none other than herself.

It took her a moment to realize her double was but a reflection. The obsidian in the cavern wall, scoured smooth by centuries of erosion, acted like a curved mirror. On its glassy surface, she could see not only a single image of herself but infinite reflections funneling to a point in the center.

When she turned her head, a moment later the reflections also turned their heads, as if following her lead. She snapped her fingers, and the reflections did the same, one after the other. Every movement she made was exactly reproduced, though slightly delayed. Inside the mirror, in all her images, Rey appeared to be the same as her physical self. It was as if she was made of an uncountable number of pieces, yet was also a singular whole.

Perhaps that was what Luke had meant when he had spoken about the Force. It was like a mirror, reflecting outward and inward, connecting everything with itself in the paradox of life.

But there was something else here. Somewhere in that chain of reflections lay the secret of her past, the secret of her parents. She had seen it in her nightmares. Now she had to look inside herself to pull it out.

"Show me," she said. "Show me who they are. Please."

She extended a hand to the dark glass. A fog spread across the surface, dissipating to present one reflection instead of thousands. The hand of Rey's reflection followed Rey's physical hand. Their fingers neared yet could never completely touch, stymied by stone.

Rey dropped her hand. The thousand other reflections returned to haunt the obsidian, dropping their hands as she did. The only secret the mirror revealed was that despite her infinite reflections, she was most definitely alone.

She closed her eyes. Though she couldn't see them, she imagined the other reflections did the same.

At least her tears were real.

CHAPTER
15

AHCH-TO had two suns but one moon. That night it hung giant and full in the sky, its eerie light shimmering in the rain on the temple's mountain ledge, where Luke stood.

He placed his hands on the meditation stone on which Rey had sat a few hours before. He could still feel her there, specks and motes of her presence drifting in the currents of the past. But he wasn't concerned with her. He had another in mind.

Luke shut his eyes and breathed. The patter of raindrops and sloshing of the tides soothed him as he let the Force take him where he needed to go.

His mind's eye opened to see Leia, lying on a bed on a star cruiser, hooked up to medical devices. She was near death, her life clinging to the Force. His touch stirred her awake.

"Luke?"

Her presence in the Force brightened. The medical readouts showed increased signs of activity. Luke strained to hold the connection. He had not communicated with his sister for a long time, and they had grown apart, not only as siblings but also in the Force.

"Leia," he said, and bestowed to her what strength of his he could before the connection faded for good.

When he opened his eyes, he saw with a new clarity. It wasn't the galaxy that needed him. It was his sister. She was hurt.

He hurried down into the village, his robes drenched by the storm. "Rey, you were right. I'm coming with you," he said loudly. "Rey?"

No one answered him. But a light shone in the doorway of her hut. He heard voices.

Luke went up to the door and looked inside. Rey sat on the ground, talking to someone Luke could not see.

"All those years in the desert on Jakku, all that time, I had never felt so alone," she said.

"You're not alone."

Luke braced himself at the second voice. He heard it through the Force. Ben Solo—or Kylo Ren as he now called himself—was communing with Rey.

"Neither are you," Rey replied. "It isn't too late." She extended a hand, then bent her fingers, as if clasping the hand of another.

Luke strode into the hut, intruding on their shared vision. The Force revealed that his disgraced pupil had locked his hand with Rey's. The two were in league.

"Stop!" Luke gestured at the walls and ceiling of the hut. All the stone blocks shot outward, as if detonated. Ben looked at Luke, then disappeared. Rey gripped air where she had been holding Ben's hand.

She rose, now wet from the rain since the hut had lost its roof. "Is it true? Did you try to murder him?"

"Leave this island. *Now*." Luke began to walk away. He would find another way to help Leia. The girl could not be trusted.

"No—you answer me. Tell me the truth!"

Luke didn't stop. That this girl had the gall to even suggest—

He fell, the back of his skull ringing in agony. She'd struck him from behind. Rolling in the mud, he looked up, his head throbbing. Rey hovered over him, wielding her staff.

"Did you do it? Did you create Kylo Ren by trying to kill Ben?"

Luke staved off the pounding pain and staggered back to his feet. He started to shuffle away. She swung again.

This time he was ready.

Calling on the Force, he snapped a lightning rod off the roof of a hut and brought it flying into his hand. He used it to parry Rey's assault, then pushed her off her feet. She bounded up, undeterred, whirling her staff for another blow. Their weapons clanged against each other, battering out a rhythm with every strike. Her aggressiveness surprised him, as did her talent, and she drove him backward. But retreat did not signal defeat.

Blocking her attacks, Luke levered the other end of his

rod to swing it back at her like a pendulum. Her staff flew from her grip. She was weaponless.

But not for long.

She summoned his old lightsaber from her satchel, activated it, and slashed. The blue blade sliced through the lightning rod and Luke tumbled to the ground.

She held the lightsaber over him. Rain sizzled against its energy beam. But she didn't strike. She switched the saber off. "Tell me the truth."

Luke wheezed from the fight. He knew he couldn't hold on to the past any longer. And he wasn't Obi-Wan. He couldn't tell things from "a certain point of view," as his first Jedi teacher had excused the half-truths he had told about Luke's father. Luke couldn't lie.

"I saw darkness," Luke said. He fixed his thoughts on the memory that never went away, that fateful moment when he had entered Ben's quarters.

He remembered holding his hand over his sleeping nephew, then closing his eyes as he searched Ben's mind.

"I had sensed the darkness building in him. I had seen it in moments during his training. But then I looked inside, and it was beyond what I ever imagined."

Horrible thoughts that weren't his own bubbled up like splattering lava. Ben screamed, Ben shrieked, Ben killed, Ben changed. A blue lightsaber replaced by a crackling red one. Still, Luke kept himself rooted in the memory, as much as it caused him pain. "Snoke had already turned his heart. He would bring destruction and pain and death and the end of everything I loved because of what he would become. And for the briefest moment of pure instinct, I thought I could stop it."

In that memory, he unbuckled his lightsaber from his belt. He activated it and looked at the green beam, but did not raise it to deliver a killing stroke. Nevertheless, for an instant, he considered the possibility. Ben was completely vulnerable on his pallet.

"It passed like a fleeting shadow. And I was left with shame."

Ben woke to find Luke clutching his lightsaber hilt. Recognition of the deed Luke had contemplated poisoned his stare.

"The last thing I saw were the eyes of a frightened boy whose master had failed him."

Ben called his own saber to him, igniting it in an attack. Luke raised his in defense, and the two swords crackled and clashed.

"No, Ben!"

But nothing Luke could say or do would ever restore his nephew's trust in him. The young man lifted a hand and the ceiling collapsed on his uncle in a pile of rubble.

A warm hand on his arm pulled Luke away from the memory. He found himself back on Ahch-To, with Rey kneeling beside him in the mud. "You failed him by thinking his choice was made," she said. "It wasn't. There's still conflict in him. If he were turned from the dark side, that could shift the tide. This could be how we win."

Luke shook his head. "This is not going to go the way you think."

"It is. Just now, when we touched hands, I saw his future. I *saw* it, as solid as I'm seeing you. If I go to him, Ben Solo will turn," Rey said.

"I killed Ben Solo that night, if not in body, then in spirit. Now there is only Kylo Ren, and he's stronger than you know, Rey." He looked up at the girl, beseeching her to listen to him. "Don't do this."

Rey rose and held out Luke's old lightsaber to him, as she had when she'd first approached him on the cliff. He admired her persistence, but he knew that she alone wouldn't be enough. One person was never enough, it seemed, to dispel the darkness. Luke brought his father back to the light, but Darth Vader's evil returned to possess Luke's own nephew. The cycle of light and darkness was inevitable, just as the moon of Ahch-To would overtake the suns.

He refused the lightsaber.

"Then he's our last hope," Rey said. She stalked away from him, heading in the direction of the *Falcon*.

Luke rose, shaking off the mud and the pain. This time, it was he who followed her, down the mountainside. If she heard him, she didn't turn in acknowledgment.

Luke halted at the bottom of the staircase. Chewbacca was visible in the *Falcon*'s cockpit. He saw Luke and waved for him to come aboard. Luke shook his head. He worried that the Wookiee might run out and try to wrangle him inside the ship. But Chewbacca just bared his fangs and looked away from Luke, busying himself with the controls from his co-pilot's seat.

The *Falcon* thrummed, preparing for takeoff. Water ran down its sides in rivulets. A curious R2-D2 sheltered underneath the ship, waiting for Rey at the ramp. She ignored his queries and strode up into the freighter without a word. Some wayward porgs toddled after her.

Luke wanted to pull her back, but he knew that was pointless. Had he not done the same as her when he had cut short his Jedi training on Dagobah and gone off to save his friends? Rey would have to learn her own lessons, as he had.

R2-D2 rolled after Rey on his treads. But at the base of the ramp, the droid stopped, swiveled his dome, and focused his radar eye on Luke.

Beep?

Luke mustered a smile. "Thank you for everything, old buddy. You were right to show me that message. Send my best to Threepio."

The ramp started to lift. R2-D2 whined and rocked from leg to leg. The droid would have dropped off the ramp if Luke hadn't held up a hand. "You must stay with the girl. Make sure she gets back to safety."

The ramp continued to rise. R2-D2 kept rocking. Luke struggled to maintain his own composure.

"May the Force be with you, Artoo."

The last Luke saw of his loyal companion was the indicator light on the astromech's dome blinking red in the rain.

As the hatch closed, a small, sad sound pierced through the rumble of the freighter's engines.

Meeep.

Luke bowed his head and walked back up the stairs.

From a nearby cliff, he watched the *Millennium Falcon* vanish into the clouds. Rain trickled from his beard, his brow, and even his eyes.

Though he had escaped the rubble of the temple he had built, its weight remained.

CHAPTER

16

WHEN the Mega-Destroyer obliterated the *Anodyne* and the *Ninka*, Poe reached a quick and necessary conclusion.

He had to save the Resistance—from itself.

He stepped up his pace to the cruiser's secondary bridge. Flares lit the corridor, since most power for unessential systems had been redirected to the engines. The *Raddus* was burning through its last reserves of fuel, and once the tanks were empty, it would slow down and the First Order armada would destroy the cruiser just as it had the other two ships. Vice Admiral Holdo's plan, if she even had a plan, wasn't working.

Commander D'Acy blocked Poe at the doorway. "The admiral has banned you from the bridge. Let's not have a scene."

"Let's." Poe pushed past her onto the bridge.

Holdo looked up from a monitor. "Flyboy."

Poe did not salute. "Cut it. We had a fleet, now we're

down to one ship and you've told us nothing. Tell us that we have a plan, that we have hope. Please."

Holdo stood tall. "When I served under Leia, she'd say hope is like the sun. If you only believe in it when you can see it—"

"You'll never make it through the night," Poe finished. General Organa had offered him the same proverb when he had joined the Resistance.

An image of an ovoid loadlifter ship appeared on a screen near him, and Poe realized what she had in mind. "You're fueling up the transports. All of them."

Holdo neither confirmed nor denied.

"We're abandoning ship? That's what you've got?" Poe asked. "That's what you've brought us to? Coward! The transports are unshielded, unarmed. We abandon this cruiser, we don't stand a chance!"

"Captain—"

Poe didn't let her talk. "This will destroy the Resistance. You're not just a coward. You're a traitor!"

Holdo turned to her security officers. "Get this man off my bridge."

The officers pulled Poe out the door. He didn't put up a fight. In the corridor, he held up his hands and told the security officers he would go with them peacefully. Out of respect, they didn't cuff him, and he walked with them to the hangar. Some transports had a brig for prisoners. He'd probably spend the last minutes of his life in a cell.

As they turned a corner, Lieutenant Connix and a group of six starfighter pilots, one of them Poe's squadron mate C'ai Threnalli, stepped out before them. "We'll take Dameron from here," Connix said.

The security officers backed away. No blasters were pulled. Connix and her contingent directed Poe into a maintenance room, where he was handed a comlink.

"What's going on?" Poe asked.

A female voice crackled over the comlink. "Captain Dameron, is that you?"

It took Poe a second to identify the speaker. "Rose?"

"Hold on." The volume of her voice lowered, as if she was turning her head. "Finn, get up here! I got through to the fleet. Poe's on the line!"

Moments later, Finn spoke over the comm. "Poe, we're on our way back!"

"Holdo's loading the crew into shuttles. She's going to abandon ship," Poe said. "Where are you?"

"We're on our way back to the fleet. We're so close."

"Did you find the Master Codebreaker?" Poe asked.

"We found . . . ah . . . a . . . codebreaker," Finn said, without much confidence. "But I promise we can shut the tracker down. Just buy us a little more time!

Poe looked at Threnalli and the others. They were on his side, willing to do whatever was necessary to save the Resistance.

"All right," Poe said to Finn. "Hurry!"

———

Rey opened the locker under the medbed in the *Millennium Falcon*'s lounge. Before they had departed Ahch-To, she had taken a few things from the world she deemed important, and these she stowed inside the locker. She thought they might be of use in the future to her or someone like her in case she didn't make it back from where she was going. Because the more she thought about where she was going, the more she feared she wouldn't make it back.

On the journey away from Ahch-To, she had R2-D2 input the coordinates from her binary beacon into the navi-computer. The droid had beeped that it could be dangerous to go there. There were reports of the First Order fleet in that region of space. That only strengthened her resolve. She needed to go wherever Kylo Ren could be.

Maybe she was delusional to be doing this. Maybe the goodness she'd felt when she had touched Ren's hand was nothing more than wishful thinking.

She tried to hide her apprehension from Chewbacca and R2-D2 as they gathered in the *Falcon*'s escape pod bay. That proved even harder when she saw the pods resembled funeral caskets. She could be sentencing herself to death.

"As soon as I launch, you jump back out of range and stay there till you get my signal," she said to Chewie.

The Wookiee yowled, disapproving of her plan. But she was grateful he didn't try to stop her. He helped her get into the pod. "If you see Finn before I do, tell him . . ." She faltered, unable to find the words she wanted to say.

Chewbacca nodded and ruffed.

"Yeah, perfect. Tell him that." She conformed her body to the interior of the pod, then raised a thumb. Chewbacca closed the hatch.

The Wookiee shambled off to the cockpit, but R2-D2 stayed in the bay. Through the pod's window, she saw his big red photoreceptor focused on her. She grinned a good-bye.

When the *Falcon* exited hyperspace, Rey's pod was jettisoned toward the First Order armada and its Mega-Destroyer. The *Falcon* did not tarry and shot back to lightspeed.

It was now Rey all alone against the mighty First Order.

Seated in the pilot's chair of the space yacht *Libertine*, Rose pulled the lightspeed lever to exit hyperspace. Huddled around her were Finn, BB-8, and the fast-talking jack-of-all-trades who called himself DJ, after the initials of his cap's slogan, "Don't join." Rose doubted this nickname was anywhere close to his real name, if he still remembered it. But he had rescued them, so she didn't ask any probing questions.

She did ask about the yacht, however, and BB-8 revealed that DJ had stolen it. The ball droid beeped that he had met the thief while looking for Rose and Finn in the jail. DJ had been so impressed by how BB-8 had stopped the prison guards by shooting credit chips at them that he told the droid he'd been in the same cell as BB-8's friends. The two then went off to the Canto Bight spaceport to obtain a ship and find Finn and Rose.

Normally, Rose would have ordered that they return the craft, but the *Libertine*'s database indicated the previous owner had trafficked in weapons to profit off the war, so she didn't feel guilty about putting the ship to better use.

As the blue streaks of hyperspace resolved into a fleet of First Order Star Destroyers, Rose realized that this probably wasn't better use.

"Four parsecs to go. This thing really cooks," Finn said.

Rose centered the ship's approach trajectory on the Mega-Destroyer. "I just hope we're in time. You can actually do this, right?" she asked DJ.

"Yeah, about that. Guys, I can do it. But there exists a pre-'do it' conversation about price."

"Once we're done, the Resistance will give you what-ever you want." Rose wasn't sure if that would be the case, or if the Resistance had any credits to dole out. But just as Captain Dameron had transmitted them the current coordinates of the Destroyers, she knew he'd make a strong argument to the Resistance leadership to pay the thief—if they all survived.

DJ wasn't having any of it. "What'cha got deposit-wise?" His gaze strayed to the medallion on her necklace. "Is that Haysian smelt? *That's* something."

Rose's hand went to cover her medallion. It was her last link to her sister, not something she could barter away. Finn spoke up for her. "No. You've got our word that you're gonna get paid. That should be enough."

"Guys, I want to keep helping," DJ said. "But no some-thing, n-no doing."

Sizing up the Destroyers in the armada, Rose thought of her sister. Paige would have been upset if Rose held on to the medallion when she might have saved the Resistance. Paige had died for more than a piece of jewelry.

Rose yanked the medallion off the chain and threw it to the thief. "Do it," she said.

CHAPTER
17

LUKE would have melted into the night but for the flaming torch he held. It lit his way up the cliff to the giant tree, where he would do what he should have done long before.

Before he entered the trunk, he felt a presence from the past appear behind him. "Master Yoda," Luke said.

Small and green, with pointy ears, playful eyes, and wisps of white hair, the wizened old goblin leaned on a walking stick and grinned. "Young Skywalker," he croaked, as if decades hadn't passed since he'd last seen Luke on Dagobah.

Luke knew such time didn't amount to much in Yoda's lifespan, but to Luke it seemed like an eternity. And during that eternity Luke had come to a grim realization. Yoda and Obi-Wan might have forged him into a weapon to fight the Emperor and Darth Vader, yet they had failed to equip him with the knowledge to stamp out the darkness for good. Their belief in the return of the Jedi had led Luke to err in his teaching and produce another Darth Vader in Kylo Ren.

"I'm ending all of this. I'm going to burn it down. Don't try to stop me," Luke said, holding his torch high.

Yoda didn't try anything. He shuffled aside, putting up no defense at all.

Luke stepped toward the tree, grappling with what he was about to do. A single lick of flame would burn down millennia of scholarship. The history of the Jedi, their secret lore and ancient wisdom, would be gone. Not because some evil emperor or dark lord had destroyed them, but because he, Luke Skywalker, had decided such knowledge was best not learned.

He had been preparing himself to do this for years. Yet now he couldn't.

Yoda snuffed in annoyance, just as he had on Dagobah when Luke failed one of his lessons. He lifted a gnarled finger toward the tree. Lightning shot forth and hit the trunk to do what Luke could not.

The library began to burn.

Guilt suddenly seized Luke's heart. What had his old master done? He dropped his torch and tried to smother the fire with his robes while Yoda cackled. "Yee-hee-hee—ending this all I am—ho-ho-ho-ho! Oh, Skywalker, missed you I have!"

Luke rushed toward the hollow in a vain effort to salvage what he could. But the fire roared at him, preventing him from entering.

He retreated from the blaze. There was nothing he could do. And if Yoda had permitted it, perhaps Luke hadn't been so wrong in his decision after all. "So it *is* time, for the Jedi Order to end."

"Time it is," Yoda said, "for you to look past a shelf of old books."

"But the sacred texts . . ." Branches fell from the tree and the fire blazed like a funeral pyre, consuming everything within. Luke hadn't expected to regret the library's loss, but regret it he did.

"Read them have you? Page-turners they were not," Yoda said.

Luke peered down at the diminutive creature. Was he truly the ghost of the Jedi Master who had once led the Council and gone into hiding to save the Order? Or was he just a figment of Luke's imagination?

"Skywalker, Skywalker," Yoda said with a heavy sigh, "still looking to the horizon. Never *here*. Never *now*. The need in front of your nose." He dinged his walking stick on the bridge of Luke's nose. "Wisdom the books held, and goodness the Jedi Order has, but these are not what the girl Rey needed. Needed a master, she did."

Luke was loath to admit it, but the tiny Jedi Master had a point. Luke had been so stubborn—so set in his ways about ending the Jedi for good—that he hadn't allowed himself to become a mentor to her like Yoda had been to him.

"The Jedi failed. I . . . failed, Master Yoda," he said, closing his eyes for a moment. "I was weak. Unwise. I can't be what she needs me to be."

"Heeded my words not, did you? 'Pass on what you have

learned,'" Yoda said, repeating the words he had uttered on his deathbed. "Wisdom, yes. But folly also. Strength and mastery, *hmph*, but weakness and failure—yes! Failure most of all. The greatest teacher, failure is. Learned this you have not."

Yoda might as well have been talking about himself. Was the Jedi Order's failure to stop the rise of the Empire why Yoda had fled to a swamp planet rather than return to confront the Emperor? If Yoda, with his talent in the Force, had led the fight from the outset, he could have reestablished the Jedi and saved the galaxy so much pain.

Yet Yoda had not incited more war. He had retreated in defeat. *Wars not make one great*, he'd told Luke when they'd first met. His exile had allowed the galaxy—in the guise of young Luke Skywalker—to come to him.

Luke had followed Yoda's example by secluding himself on Ahch-To. He had accepted failure and defeat, but what he hadn't accepted was the idea of forgiving himself. He'd made mistakes in teaching Ben Solo, yet that didn't mean what he had taught was wrong, or even that Rey would follow in Ben's path. Good teachers were not tyrants. They could not control how the students used the knowledge they were taught. Teachers could only pass on what they themselves had learned. For hadn't Yoda taught him, despite knowing the sins of his father, Anakin Skywalker? The Jedi Master had never given up on the hope that every student, no matter their background, could apply what they learned to bring light into the universe.

"We are what they grow beyond." Nine centuries of wrinkles furrowed Yoda's brow. "That is the true burden of all masters."

The heat from the flames scorched Luke's skin, but he did not move away. When the morning came and the fires had died, Luke watched the smoke curl and vanish from the husk of the tree.

He stood alone.

CHAPTER
18

KYLO REN inspected the capsule that TIE fighters had ferried into the Mega-Destroyer's hangar. It was labeled ESCAPE POD CLASS A940—*MILLENNIUM FALCON* above scribbling that read *Property of Han Solo—please return!*

It amused Ren that nothing could be returned to Han Solo anymore.

The hatch opened in a cloud of vapor and Rey emerged. Ren took her arm and helped her forward. She tensed but did not wrest her arm free. He let it go on his own.

"I've been waiting for you," he said. "As you are now a prisoner of the First Order, regulations require we do a brisk search."

"I have nothing to hide," Rey said.

Two stormtroopers stepped forward and shackled her hands with binders. Then they patted her down and searched the contents of her satchel. A lightsaber was produced.

Ren smirked. "Nothing?"

"You mentioned to me that was *yours*."

"Yes, I believe I did." Ren took the lightsaber from the trooper with a smile. "Come with me, Rey from Jakku."

He escorted her to the turbolift, with the troopers marching in lockstep behind her. When the lift doors hissed opened, he gestured Rey inside and motioned the troopers to leave. Entering the turbolift, Ren keyed in a special code on the floor selector. The doors closed and the lift rose.

"Snoke?" Rey asked.

Ren said nothing and examined the lightsaber. He had been searching for it for years. His grandfather had built it, yet Obi-Wan Kenobi had stolen it and passed it down to Luke. Now it was his.

"You don't have to do this," Rey said. "I feel the conflict in you, growing since you killed Han. It's tearing you apart."

He laughed. "Is that why you came? To tell me about my conflict?"

"No. Look at me." Her voice softened. "Ben."

He looked at her. She stood confident, seemingly unafraid. What had Luke taught her? Surely not much, in the few days she'd been with him.

"When we touched, I saw your future," Rey said. "Just the shape of it, but solid and clear. You will not bow before Snoke. You will turn. I'll help you. I *saw* it. It's your destiny."

"You're wrong. When we touched, I saw something, too. Not your future—your *past*. And because of what I saw, I know that when the moment comes, you'll be the one to turn. You'll stand with me, Rey." He saved his strongest venom for last. "I saw who your parents are."

It hit her like he'd wanted it to—a shock to her heart. Dread quashed the confidence in her eyes. He almost felt sad for her.

Almost.

The doors parted. Ren led the girl out into the cavernous hall. The Praetorian Guards maintained their positions, four to each side of the throne occupied by the Supreme Leader. Ren dropped to a knee before him.

"Well done, my good apprentice. My faith in you is restored." Snoke blessed Ren with a grin as his gaze locked on Rey. "Young Rey, welcome."

Kylo Ren sensed nothing from the girl but fear.

The conspirators waylaid Vice Admiral Holdo in the hangar. She was clearly surprised that Poe wasn't in custody, and he didn't waste the moment. He informed her that Rose and Finn were trying to disable the *Supremacy*'s hyperspace tracker.

"They're doing *what*?"

"They're trying to save us!" Poe said. "This is our best hope of escape. You have to give Finn and Rose all the time you can."

Holdo grew livid. "They've bet the survival of the Resistance on bad odds, just to be heroes—and you with them?" She addressed the crew running around the converted cargo shuttles. "We need to get clear of this cruiser. Load the transports!"

The hangar doors opened in preparation for launch. C'ai Threnalli glanced at Poe, giving him the signal.

"I was afraid you'd say that," Poe told Holdo. He didn't want to do what he was about to do, but what choice did he have? He drew his blaster and turned it on the vice admiral, as did Threnalli, Lieutenant Connix, and the rest of the group. "Admiral Holdo, I'm relieving you of your duty, for the survival of the ship, its crew, and the Resistance."

Holdo lifted her hands, glowering at Poe. Her staff also surrendered. "I hope you understand what you're doing, Dameron," she said.

Poe turned to Threnalli. "I'm going to the bridge. If they move, stun 'em."

As he raced out of the hangar, the implications of what he had done began to sink in.

He had just staged a mutiny.

Finn held his breath while the *Libertine* drifted toward the Mega-Destroyer *Supremacy*. At any moment they might be blasted into space debris. DJ didn't seem to be worried. Before they had emerged from hyperspace, he had inserted a tool into the yacht's controls that he claimed would make the ship invisible from the First Order's scopes. But Finn had heard so many stories about overhyped cloaking devices, none of which actually worked, that he doubted this one would. If cloaking your ship was easy as DJ made it out to be, everybody would own one of these magical gadgets. Yet

Finn didn't raise a stink when a flight of TIEs zoomed past the *Libertine* without pause. Maybe DJ's tool wasn't as unrealistic as it seemed.

Finn breathed more easily once the yacht penetrated the *Supremacy*'s shields. DJ might not have been the Master Codebreaker Maz had recommended, but he was no slouch. He hacked into the Mega-Destroyer's deflector shield timer and programmed a gap in the coverage so they could slip through it. Finn recalled how Han Solo had infiltrated Starkiller Base by exploiting a similar timing gap in the shields, but Han had crashed his beloved *Millennium Falcon* on the planet below. Fortunately, they weren't accelerating at a speed that would cause that kind of mishap. Rose glided the *Libertine* into the *Supremacy*'s exhaust nozzle and docked against a maintenance hatch, all without seeming to attract the First Order's notice.

Their crazy plan was working—so far.

Disembarking from the yacht, BB-8 took point and rolled down the repair shaft, mapping and scanning the area. Finn crawled after the droid with Rose and DJ, though Rose soon halted before a ventilation duct that was covered in lint. She started to pry loose the grill. "Our way in."

Once the grill was freed, they wormed through the duct and out into a hot room that smelled of soap. Officers' uniforms advanced on a conveyer belt, where a droid with iron-hot limbs steam-pressed the clothes into neatly folded packets.

Finn shot Rose a quizzical look. "The laundry room?"

"Time to dress the part, gentlemen," she said.

It made sense. They wouldn't have to sneak around as much if they looked like they belonged here. "Remember to tuck in your shirts," Finn said. "The First Order doesn't tolerate wrinkles."

They took clothing packets in their sizes and changed behind the cleaning tubs. Finn missed the roominess of Poe's flight jacket, which he had stowed back on the yacht. The drab uniform he now wore was starch stiff and itched. The cap gave him a headache and the belt squeezed his guts. Why did the First Order have a knack for making things uncomfortable?

For BB-8's disguise, Finn found a black waste bucket and turned it over on top of the astromech. If no one looked too close, BB-8 could be mistaken for a mouse droid.

To reach the engineering section where Rose could disable the tracker, they had to board a turbolift at the other end of an operations center. So they held their chins high and strode through a warren of computer consoles, holographic displays, and targeting systems. First Order officers patrolled the stations, barking commands at analysts. One lieutenant put a datapad in front of Rose. "Captain, could you okay this?"

She gave the lieutenant's datapad a once-over, then snapped "okay" and walked onward with Finn and DJ, as if she were on more important business. BB-8 received more attention from the mouse droids zipping about, yet other than some inquisitive beeps, none sounded an alert.

As they neared the turbolifts, one of the senior-ranking officers cast a curious glance at them. "This isn't working," whispered DJ.

Finn kept his gaze forward. "Almost there."

Arriving at the lifts, Rose summoned a car with a button. The doors opened and they all went inside to join a half dozen stormtroopers. The senior officer began to hurry toward them. Rose had trouble with the controls. Two stormtroopers looked at each other. Sweat pooled under Finn's tight collar. Was this how everything was going to end? The officer had gotten within a few steps when the lift doors finally shut and the car moved.

Levels whooshed past the windows. No one spoke. But a trooper turned his helmet toward Finn and stared at him. DJ dangled his hand near his holster. Finn had to do something or the thief might get trigger-happy.

Finn shot the trooper a dirty look. "Is there a problem, soldier?"

"Eff-Enn-Two-One-Eight-Seven?" The trooper's comm filter couldn't suppress his surprise, nor could the vacant expression of his helmet.

Finn recognized the voice. The trooper was an old batch buddy who'd given him a run for top shot at target practice. But Finn played dumb.

"You don't remember me." The trooper sounded disappointed. "Nine-Two-Six, from induct camp, batch eight. But I remember you."

The other troopers started to glance at Finn and their

comrade. Rose exchanged nervous looks with DJ, who was ready to draw.

Finn leaned closer to the trooper and whispered, "Nine-Two-Six. Please . . . don't."

"Sorry, Two-One-Eight-Seven," the trooper said. "I know I'm not supposed to initiate contact with officers. But look at you! Never took you for captain material. Batch eight, hey-ho!" He slapped Finn's rear, like all the cadets used to do in training to motivate each other.

Rose shooed DJ's hand away from his blaster. The car halted and the doors opened.

Finn slapped his old buddy back. "Batch eight," he said in solidarity.

Everyone exited the turbolift. The troopers marched off in one direction, and Finn, Rose, DJ, and BB-8 went in the other. Only when they had turned down a hallway did they relax.

Finn drew some satisfaction from knowing the First Order's arrogance was what had saved them. Matters outside of combat and battle strategy were withheld from stormtroopers. Finn's batch buddy obviously never got the memo that the First Order had declared Finn a traitor.

That horrible training cycle Finn had spent mopping the Mega-Destroyer's floors finally came to good use. He led them on a run through a maze of corridors to a locked blast door. "This is it. The tracker's right behind this door."

DJ crouched over the entry console. He retrieved Rose's medallion from his pocket and pressed it into the console.

Before Rose could protest, sparks flew, and the console short-circuited.

"Haysian smelt makes the best conductor," DJ said. He tossed the medallion to Rose. "You're welcome."

"Thank you," Rose said.

Finn reconsidered the thief. Perhaps DJ wasn't as greedy as he'd thought.

As DJ continued to fiddle with the console, Rose waited beside Finn. "Good time to figure out how we get back to the fleet."

"I know where the nearest escape pods are," Finn said.

Rose snickered. "Of course you do."

Finn cringed. She'd never let him live that one down.

DJ punched buttons on the console. "Almost there . . ."

Poe's voice crackled over BB-8's speaker. "Beebee-Ate, tell me something good."

The droid ejected a comlink, which Finn caught. "Poe, we're almost there. Have the cruiser prepped for lightspeed."

"Yeah, I'm on it, pal," Poe said. "You just hurry."

"Now or never!" Finn said to DJ.

The thief looked at them. "Now," he said, and the blast doors slid open.

The room beyond was jam-packed with astronaviga-tional systems. A series of circuit breakers was installed on the back wall. Flipping those breakers would cut power to the tracker. Their crazy plan was seconds from being a success.

But it all proved to be little more than a tantalizing glimpse. A squad of stormtroopers clattered through adjoining doors, led by the senior officer who had spotted them in the operations center.

A chrome-armored trooper pushed through the ranks. "Eff-Enn-Two-One-Eight-Seven. So good to have you back."

Finn grimaced. He should've known a trash compactor would never be able to hold his former commanding officer, Captain Phasma.

CHAPTER 19

POE readied the *Raddus* for a hyperspace jump, blaster in hand. Minutes before, he had taken complete control of the bridge and sent the crew to the hangar. The only ones who stayed were Lieutenant Connix and General Organa's assistant, C-3PO.

Though more anxious than usual, the protocol droid obeyed Poe's orders, having opened up a comm channel with the team on the Mega-Destroyer through BB-8. But Finn's report that they were within reach of the tracker flustered C-3PO. "Sir, I'm almost afraid to ask, but—"

Poe had no time to argue with the droid. "Good instinct, Threepio. Go with that." As he entered hyperspace coordinates, a screen monitoring the hangar lit up with blaster fire. Holdo and her crew were fighting back, and Poe knew his small group of mutineers holding the hangar wouldn't last long.

"Seal that door!" he yelled to Connix. The lieutenant did as commanded, rushing back to a console to assist with astronavigation. But C-3PO hustled toward the door access controls.

"Threepio, stay away from that!"

"It would be quite against my programming to be a party to mutiny, Captain Dameron!" said the droid, evidently having computed what was going on. "It is not correct protocol."

The edges of the door began to glow and spark. Someone was trying to cut through it. The firefight still blazed on the screen, so Holdo's troops couldn't be behind it. Had those loyal to Poe turned against him?

C-3PO backpedaled from the door but kept talking. "I will have some very strong words in my official report when this is all over."

Poe pounded his fist on the comm button. "Finn?" There was no response. "Finn, are you there?" Where had Finn gone? *"Finn!"*

Then Poe heard cries and protests on the comm. The worst had happened. The First Order's troopers had found his friends and taken them prisoner.

It seemed like Poe would share a similar fate. A section of the bridge door clanked to the floor, melted from the other side. Keeping one hand atop the hyperspace lever, Poe raised his pistol at the intruder.

General Leia Organa ducked through the hole.

Shocked but overjoyed to see she had recovered, Poe lowered his weapon.

The general triggered hers.

A stun bolt coursed through Poe's nerves. He blacked out.

In the cavernous throne room, Rey stood petrified.

The being in the golden robes looked more dead than alive, like a cadaver animated by some evil force. He loomed large in the chair, yet his eyes were small, pinpricks of misery that froze Rey in cold terror.

This was the Supreme Leader of the First Order, the one known as Snoke.

He curled a finger and the shackles around her wrists released to clang on the floor. "Come closer, child."

Summoning every iota of will, she refused.

"So much strength," he said. "Darkness rises, and light to meet it. I warned my young apprentice that as he grew stronger, his equal in the light would rise."

Kylo Ren continued to kneel, even as Luke's lightsaber was torn from his grasp and shot into Snoke's hand.

The Supreme Leader studied the weapon. "That light was Skywalker, I assumed," he said, "wrongly."

He placed the hilt on the arm of his chair, then motioned to Rey. "Closer, I said."

Rey dug in her heels, but she was pulled forward against her will, past a pair of guards in red armor, until she stood at the foot of the throne. While her body would not obey her, her mind remained free.

"You underestimate Skywalker and Ben Solo," she said, with a look at Kylo Ren, "and me. It will be your downfall."

"Oh." Snoke sounded intrigued. "Have you seen something? A weakness in my apprentice? Is that why you came? Young fool. It was I who bridged your minds. I stoked Ren's conflicted soul. I knew he was not strong enough to hide it from you, and you were not strong enough to resist the bait."

As if pulled by cords, Rey was wrenched up the stairs in front of Snoke's mangled face. "Now you will give me Skywalker," he said, "then I will kill you with the cruelest stroke."

She wanted to mount a proper defense. But all she could manage was one word. "No."

Snoke smacked his thin lips. "Yes."

He flicked his hand and Rey flew off her feet, slamming into an invisible wall a few meters away. He kept her levitating high off the floor as the hideous tentacles of his mind invaded hers, contorting the flesh of her face.

"Give . . . me . . . everything!"

Snoke's tendrils slithered like snakes around her brain, and with one vicious pull seemed to yank her lobes apart. She flailed and screamed, but there was no end to the pain.

With her mind went her defiance. She gave Snoke everything.

Rose endured shoves and kicks from the stormtroopers as Captain Phasma took them into the Mega-Destroyer's hangar. Finn was roughed up even more. DJ, on the other hand, was nowhere to be seen.

The hangar offered no opportunities for revenge or

escape. The First Order's firepower was on full display with a dizzying array of TIE fighters, droid walkers, assault shuttles, and combat-ready stormtroopers. A tall and trim military officer with hay-colored hair watched over it all.

"General Hux. I have caught the intruders," Phasma said.

The man turned toward them and Rose recognized him immediately. Though Armitage Hux looked far too young to be a general, Rose knew the First Order thrived on the passion and arrogance of youth, which were Hux's chief qualities.

Hux slapped Finn across the cheek. Finn didn't flinch. "Well done, Phasma. I can't say I approve of the methods, but I can't argue with the results," Hux said.

DJ stepped out from behind a row of troopers as the sleek *Libertine* settled on the hangar floor. Flight officers guided a repulsor sled of credit crates into its hold.

"Your ship and payment, just as we agreed," Phasma said to DJ.

Rose scowled at the thief. "You lying snake!"

"We got caught," he said. "I cut a d-deal."

She regretted not trusting her instincts. DJ was just as he looked, a deceitful, flimflamming, rubbish-mouthed rat. Even his slogan "Don't join" was a lie. He had joined a side— the wrong side. And he'd pay for it, if she ever had a chance to do anything about it. "You lousy, double-crossing—"

She pounced on the traitor.

None of her swings connected before troopers restrained her. She thrashed in their grip as another officer delivered a report to Hux. "Sir, we checked on the information from the thief. Thirty Resistance transports have just launched from the cruiser."

Hux favored DJ with a half grin. "You told us the truth! Will wonders never cease?" He turned back to the officer. "Our weapons are ready?"

"Ready and aimed, sir."

Finn gave Rose a look of despair. DJ had not only sold them out, he'd sold out Poe and the whole Resistance.

"Sorry, guys," the thief said with a shrug. He went over to the credit crates.

"Fire at will," Hux told the officer.

CHAPTER
20

AFTER the stun bolt wore off, Poe received a shock of another kind. He found himself lying in the cargo hold of a transport. Through a viewport he saw the *Raddus* receding. This could only mean his attempt to jump the cruiser to lightspeed had failed. Holdo had won. The Resistance was doomed.

"Poe, look." General Organa stood with Commander D'Acy at another viewport across the hold. She motioned for Poe to join them.

Poe rose and walked over to them, taking the general's hand. Her gesture told him that any discord between them no longer existed.

Out the viewport, a white orb shone brighter and bigger than any star. "What is that?" Poe asked. "There are no systems near us."

"No charted ones, no," General Organa said. "But there are still a few shadow planets in deep space. During the days of the Rebellion we used them as hideouts."

"The mineral planet Crait," D'Acy said.

Poe noticed scant variation in the world's topography. There were no signs of seas or lakes. "There's a rebel base there?"

"Remote but heavily armored, with enough power to get a distress signal to our allies scattered in the Outer Rim," D'Acy said.

Their talk confused him. Had they forgotten about the fleet of Star Destroyers in pursuit?

The general answered before Poe could ask. "The First Order is tracking our big ship. They aren't monitoring for small transports."

Poe began to connect the dots. "So . . . we'll slip down to the surface unnoticed and hide till they pass." He thought out loud before realizing: "It'll work!" He looked at the planet and the other Resistance transports that flew toward it. "Why didn't the vice admiral tell me?"

General Organa slipped the bracelet beacon off Poe's wrist. In all the activity, he'd forgotten he was even wearing it. "The fewer who knew the better. Protecting the light was more important to her than looking like a hero."

Poe turned to the other viewport. The *Raddus* shrank in size as it led the Mega-Destroyer and its armada away from the planet.

Holdo and her crew were giving up their lives for the Resistance.

Poe felt ashamed he'd ever questioned her loyalty. She didn't just play the part of a hero, Vice Admiral Holdo *was* a hero.

The Mega-Destroyer suddenly disgorged a blinding storm of energy, not at the cruiser but past it, at the transports. The viewports automatically darkened to dim a blinding explosion.

D'Acy gasped. General Organa sighed. Poe stumbled toward the cockpit as shockwaves from other explosions rocked the transport. The First Order had foiled Holdo's plan. The Mega-Destroyer's cannons had the range to hit the transports even while tracking the cruiser.

By the time Poe reached the cockpit, fifteen of the thirty Resistance transports had been blown apart. "Give it full thrusters, full speed!"

The pilot's face was red from stress. "I am, sir, I am!"

Poe knew the pilot couldn't do much more. The transports had been designed for cargo hauling, not battle. It'd be a miracle if one transport even managed to land on the planet.

Kylo Ren averted his eyes from the mental torture Snoke was inflicting on Rey. But that didn't stop him from hearing Rey's screams. He knew the anguish of a mind being torn open and having its secrets ripped out. He'd performed the act many times himself—even on Rey after he had captured her on Takodana.

When his master had taken what he wanted, Rey fell to the ground near Ren with a bone-crunching thud. She turned over, groaning.

"Well, well, well," Snoke said, "I did not expect Skywalker to be so wise. We will give him and the Jedi Order the death he longs for. After the rebels are gone, we will go to his planet and obliterate the entire island."

The revelation startled Ren. Luke Skywalker was a coward, not someone who sought death. If he wanted out, why didn't he do it himself?

Whimpering in pain, Rey rolled on the floor, lifting her hand toward Snoke. The lightsaber flew from the throne's armrest toward her.

Snoke flicked his wrist and the lightsaber looped around Rey to club her in the skull, as if reprimanding a naughty child. The hilt then returned to the throne and settled back on the armrest.

"Such spunk. Look here now." Snoke gestured and Rey slid past the silent Praetorian Guard toward the oval oculus that peered through a gap in the red curtains. Ren stepped forward to look through the lens. What he saw thrilled him.

The Mega-Destroyer's cannons reached across the expanse to winnow out the fleeing Resistance transports. The enemy cruiser lagged far behind them, its engines sputtering.

"The entire Resistance is on those transports. Soon they will all be gone," Snoke said. "For you, all is lost."

But Rey had not surrendered herself to despair. The desert girl had more than just spunk. Her eyes burned with a silent fire.

She still had hope.

The girl raised her hand again, and so taken was Ren by her defiance, he failed to notice that she reached not toward Luke's old lightsaber but toward his. It unfastened from his belt and sprang into her hand, its fiery blade igniting.

He was an imbecile to let down his guard—and now she had embarrassed him in front of his master! He advanced on her with the Praetorians.

Snoke snickered, holding out a hand to halt them. "You have the spirit of a true Jedi," he said to Rey. With a sweep of the same hand, he flung her across the room. "And because of that, you must die."

The lightsaber flew out of her grip, retracting its blade as it landed near Ren. He did not pick it up. Rather, he awaited the inevitable punishment for his lack of awareness.

But there was no punishment, not even a scolding from his master. "My worthy apprentice," the Supreme Leader said, almost warmly, "son of darkness, heir apparent to Lord Vader, where there was conflict I now sense resolve. Where there was weakness, strength. Complete your training. Fulfill your destiny."

Ren looked down at the lightsaber. So this was it. This was the moment for which he had long waited. He'd been mistaken to think he had completed his training by killing his father. Only by killing the girl could he achieve the destiny his master foresaw.

He retrieved his lightsaber and strode toward Rey. A

single stroke was all it would take. One might even say he was being merciful, sparing her from his master's torture.

Snoke contorted his finger. The girl's arms were wrenched behind her back and she was pulled to her knees.

"Ben," she said.

"I know what I have to do," he said.

But as he looked into her eyes, he hesitated. Just as he had hesitated to launch the torpedoes that would kill his mother. Emotions churned inside him, pangs of fear and guilt he could never fully purge. They reminded him of a part of himself he had thought he destroyed—another destiny in which he had once believed, told to him by another master.

"You think he will turn? You pathetic child," Snoke said to Rey. "I cannot be betrayed. I cannot be beaten. I see his mind. I see his every intent."

Ren held out the hilt toward Rey's chest. He needn't see her die. All he had to do was ignite the blade and it would be over.

Snoke shut his eyes and kinked his mouth in a sicklelike grin. "Yes. I see him turning the lightsaber to strike true."

At that instant, Kylo Ren perceived his true destiny. It was a destiny not prophesied by any master, but a destiny he chose for himself.

He slipped his free hand behind his back and gestured. The lightsaber on the throne's armrest pivoted a quarter turn.

Snoke's eyes remained close, his grin sharpening. "And now, foolish child," he rasped, "he ignites it and kills his true enemy."

Revenge came easier than Kylo Ren had ever imagined. But a twitch of his finger and he paid back all the punishment he had suffered over the years.

On the armrest, the blue blade of Luke's lightsaber activated with a snap-hiss and stabbed Snoke straight through his waist. The Supreme Leader gasped, staring at his apprentice. Ren called on the Force again, slicing sideways with the blade and cleaving his master in two.

His master should have learned never to let down his guard.

As the halves of Snoke tumbled from the throne, Ren enjoyed a rush of dark gratification. What he should have done to Skywalker, he had done to Snoke.

He was his own master now.

The Praetorian Guards charged with their weapons. Ren sent Luke's saber spiraling to Rey. Rising, she caught the hilt and looked at him. That hope in her eyes burned even brighter now.

They turned their backs to each other and fought as one.

The *Supremacy* rumbled with each blast of its megalaser batteries. Visible through the hangar's magnetically shielded portal, tiny dots that were the Resistance transports blinked out of existence one after the other.

"Murderer!"

Though Finn struggled in the grip of stormtroopers, he directed his slur at DJ. The thief tallied the stacks of credits near his stolen ship, not the least bit offended. "Take it easy, Big F. They blow you up today, you blow them up tomorrow. It's just business."

"You're wrong," Finn spat.

DJ shrugged. "Maybe."

Seeming satisfied by the progress of the attack, General Hux turned from the portal to his prisoners. Rose's necklace caught his glance. He grabbed the crescent medallion. "The Otomok system. That brings back memories," he said, rather fondly. "You vermin may draw a little blood with a bite now and then, but we'll always win."

As if inspired by his speech, Rose leaned forward and bit Hux's hand, breaking skin. He shrieked like a whelp while stormtroopers wrested her away from him. Blood stained her teeth.

"Execute them both!" Hux shouted at Phasma. Clasping his injured hand, he hurried off.

At Phasma's nod, the troopers shoved Finn and Rose to their knees. "Blasters are too good for them. Let's make it hurt."

The troopers drew laser axes from a supply locker. The heads of the weapons hummed, vibrating at an incredible speed. Finn and Rose tried to wriggle free, to no avail. Finn looked around for BB-8 but couldn't see the droid. Maybe he would get away to tell Poe what had happened.

"On my command," Phasma said.

Finn felt a sudden bond with the villagers he'd encountered during a raid on Jakku. Those poor people had posed no threat to the First Order, yet Phasma had carried out Kylo Ren's order to shoot them all. Finn's decision not to fire with the rest of his squad was the decision that had changed his life. It was when he had finally overcome the First Order's browbeating and brainwashing and had broken with their heartless violence. It was when he had started down the path of protecting innocents rather than preserving tyranny, a path that led him to Poe, Rey, and now Rose, the first true friends he'd ever had.

If Finn was going to die now, at least he could rest well knowing he had tried to help his friends make a difference in the galaxy.

He had only one regret.

He wished he could have convinced other troopers to do the same.

CHAPTER
21

PHYSICALLY, Rey was not in fighting condition after Snoke hurled her across his throne room. Mentally, her mind throbbed like an open wound as it pieced itself back together from his invasive probe.

But in the Force, Rey had never felt stronger.

She had been right about what she'd seen. Luke had been wrong. Kylo Ren wasn't lost to them. Under his dark shell flickered a spark of light. He could be redeemed.

She joined him in combat against the guards, and they made a most formidable pair. In a blur of laser blades, one red guard fell, then another, then two more, and then a second pair. The Praetorians' weapons clattered to the ground next to their bodies while slashed curtains fluttered down like funeral shrouds.

When Rey's fourth opponent tried to decapitate her, she pirouetted and swung, cutting through his armor and knocking him down. Kylo Ren had more difficulty with the final guard. The Praetorian thrust his pole-arm at Ren from behind and pinned down Ren's lightsaber, forcing him to drop it.

"Ben!" Rey locked the activation matrix on her hilt and tossed him the blue blade. Plucking it out of the air, Ren quickly parried what would have been a mortal blow, rolling his wrist, turning the blade into the guard's helmet.

The last of the First Order's most elite warriors crumpled to lie with his comrades and Supreme Leader on the scuffed and smoking floor.

Ren caught his breath. Rey did the same. Their eyes met, and Rey saw in Kylo Ren the good person he wanted to be.

But beyond him, she also saw the massacre that was being waged in space.

She rushed to the wall where the curtains had hung. An enormous window Showed the Destroyers converging on the Resistance cruiser while the *Supremacy* continued its assault on the transports. From what she could make out, only ten remained.

She turned to Ren. "Order them to stop firing. There's still time to save the fleet!"

Ren loomed over Snoke's body with Luke's lightsaber still drawn, as if he wanted to stab his master again.

"Ben!" Rey said again.

Ren looked up from the corpse. "That's my old name."

"What?"

"It's time to let the old things die, Rey. I want you to join me." He seemed to grow in stature. "Snoke, Skywalker, the

Sith, the Jedi, the rebels—let it all die. We can rule together and bring a new order to the galaxy."

Her chest tightened. The throbbing returned to her head. The hope that had sustained her started to wither and die. This couldn't be happening. She had felt the good in him. She had seen the real Ben—Ben Solo.

"No, Ben, don't do this! Don't go this way, please!"

Ren chuckled at her plea. "Do you want to know the truth?" he asked. "About your parents?" His eyes twinkled, cruel and sinister. "Or have you always known, and have just hidden it away, hidden it from yourself?"

She didn't want to listen to him. She wanted him to stop the charade and return to Leia. But she also wanted to know.

"Let it go," he said. "You know the truth. Say it."

She knew only what she feared. And what she feared was the truth of the voice from her dreams—the dreams that had haunted her since the day her parents abandoned her on Jakku.

Stay here. I'll come back for you, sweetheart. I promise.

That was not the voice of her mother or her father, as she had long convinced herself.

The voice was her own.

She had imagined that voice and repeated those words over and over as a child until they became part of her reality, even her dreams. They had helped her fall asleep on a hungry stomach and pushed her to persevere when the future seemed bleak. When the years went by and her parents never returned to take her back, she never gave up the hope that someday soon they would and the nightmare of her youth would be over.

It was a false hope.

Was that what Luke had tried to prompt her to confess in the library? The truth she had locked in her heart and had never let herself admit? The truth that her parents were not hardworking space merchants trying to scrape enough together to make a better life for their family?

"They were nobody," Rey said at last.

"They were filthy junk traders who sold you off for drinking money," Kylo Ren said, spitting out the words. "They're dead in a pauper's grave on Jakku, like all the other junk buried there."

Rey hadn't known those details, but she had no doubt what Kylo Ren said was true. Her whole life had been one giant lie of her own making, a castle of dreams and echoes that had no foundation.

She shook all over. She might have survived Snoke's mental thrashing, but this self-admission could break her for good.

Ren stepped toward her. "You have no place in the story. You come from nothing. You are nothing." His tone became tender. "But not to me."

He deactivated the blade. "Join me. Please." He held out his hand to her.

She looked at him, pale and ghostly in the starlight of the window. His request was sincere. He wanted to teach her. She could learn great power from him. He could help her attain her true potential in the Force. Her past didn't matter. All that mattered was her place in the future.

Rey reached out to Ren. He smiled.

Their hands never met.

Rey could never join with him. Not as he stood before her now. For he, too, had tried to erase his past, reinventing himself in the mold of his grandfather. The difference was that he had lost hope in his parents, while she had kept hope in hers, however false, alive.

Perhaps that was the very meaning of hope. It seemed false until it happened.

And if she wanted to save Ben, she would have to stop Kylo Ren.

With a tug of the Force, she summoned Luke's lightsaber from Ren's grasp. It shot toward her, then stopped. Ren raised a hand and the lightsaber froze in midair.

Rey pulled at the lightsaber with the Force, wiggling it closer to her, until Kylo Ren yanked it back toward him. Brows sweat and veins bulged as both tried to pry the lightsaber away. What Rey possessed in will, Ren matched in anger. Neither could overpower the other and lay claim to the sword.

Anakin Skywalker, Luke's father, had built this lightsaber to last. And last it had, withstanding the battles of the Clone Wars, the sands of Tatooine, the ice storms of Hoth, and the gas clouds of Bespin. Yet under the duress of the twin forces of Rey and Ren who wrenched at it like gravitational giants, the saber could not hold.

It was, after all, an elegant weapon for a more civilized age.

Under this most uncivilized pressure, the lightsaber split in two, exploding in a blaze of blinding white.

Poe hurried back into the hold. The viewport showed a handful of transports left, yet it was unlikely any would make it to the planet before the Mega-Destroyer had obliterated them all.

He thought they'd been hit when the transport rattled violently. He grabbed a handle to steady himself. Pieces of fuselage whipped past the viewport. The megalaser cannons hadn't struck them, but their neighbor, and they flew through the wreckage.

From Poe's calculations, the Resistance was down to six transports. Even if they locked themselves in the rebel base on Crait, it was not a force adequate to repel the First Order.

Lieutenant Connix stood across from him, peering out a porthole facing starboard. "Our cruiser's priming her hyperspace engines! She's running away!"

Poe stumbled over to the window. The cruiser's engines flared a hot blue-white, as they did before a leap. But he also noticed the *Raddus*'s forward bow was pointed in a direction that did not suggest retreat.

"No, she isn't," Poe said.

The *Raddus* jumped to hyperspace, but it was a short jump. A very short jump.

The cruiser emerged to slice through the Mega-Destroyer.

Like a star turning in on itself, the colossal warship buckled and burned, igniting a wave of devastation that enveloped anything near it. The *Raddus* was devoured, as were half the Destroyers in the First Order armada.

Vice Admiral Holdo had just sacrificed herself to save the Resistance.

The crew in the transport's hold cheered. But General Organa remained solemn, as did Poe.

Finn and Rose were on that Mega-Destroyer.

CHAPTER
22

"KILL them both."

Finn felt the whoosh of the axe stroke after Phasma uttered her command. But the vibrating blade never cut into his neck. A shockwave pitched him off his knees.

He must have lost consciousness, because the next thing he knew, Rose was pulling him by his leg as she had on the *Raddus*. He shook himself free. "I'm okay," he said, getting up.

Smoke stung his eyes. Alarms blared at ear-piercing decibels. The hangar around him was in shambles. Docking rigs had caved in on TIE fighters. Stormtroopers were strewn about, their armor charred and broken. Slag marked where a gunship had sat. Walkers lay toppled, their legs smashed. Fires raged everywhere.

The Mega-Destroyer had been hit hard. And from the looks of what was happening in the hangar, it was in its death throes.

Finn stumbled after Rose toward a shuttle that hadn't

sustained much damage. BB-8 rolled ahead of them, having cast off the waste bin cover. Finn didn't know how the droid had gotten there exactly, but it was just like him to join them at the last moment.

DJ was also nearby, on the verge of departure. The thief stood on the ramp of the stolen yacht, waving farewell as the ramp retracted. Finn snatched a blaster rifle from a fallen trooper and fired at the traitor. But the hatch had already closed so that the bolt glanced harmlessly off the *Libertine*'s hull.

Secondary explosions ripped through fuel lines, and dark clouds billowed across the hangar. Rose grabbed Finn's arm and he dumped the heavy rifle as they ran toward the shuttle.

Captain Phasma and a squad of stormtroopers stepped out of the smoke in front of them. Finn paled as the troopers raised their blasters.

A salvo of laser fire beat the troopers to their triggers, causing them to scatter for cover. Cannons ablaze, the head shell of a two-legged walker came off its body, showing BB-8 in the cockpit. The droid must have circumvented the walker's programming and taken control. Finn would have to thank the pesky unit if they all made it out alive.

Rose retrieved a blaster and ducked behind a melted beam, returning fire. Phasma, however, charged at Finn.

From the floor, Finn picked up a discarded riot baton and swung at Phasma, chopping off the barrel of her rifle.

Dropping the gun, she slid a quicksilver rod from her belt and pushed a button. Its ends extended into a slim baton with two needle-sharp points.

"You were never anything more than a bug in the system," she said.

Finn gripped his baton with both hands. "Let's go, chrome dome."

It wasn't a fair fight. Not only was Phasma suited in armor, but she was a master with the baton. Her strikes thundered against Finn's baton, rattling his arms and bones. All Finn could manage was to block and parry her attacks as she drove him under the walker's leg and through the smoke to a cleft in the floor. "You were always disobedient, disrespectful," she said, whirling her baton. "Your emotions make you weak!"

She hammered at his baton, and Finn could keep his balance no more. He tumbled backward into the hole. Fires crackled beneath him, but he didn't fall far. He landed on the platform of a cargo lift. The platform's repulsors still functioned and he dialed them to take himself back up to the hangar.

Phasma hadn't expected him to reemerge, and that mistake cost her. Finn clocked his baton at her helmet, sending her sprawling to the hangar floor.

When she lifted her head, he saw her helmet had been cracked. A blue eye looked back at him. He had never thought of Captain Phasma without her helmet, and seeing that she was actually human made him shudder.

"You were always scum," Phasma said.

Finn nodded. "*Rebel* scum."

The floor beneath Phasma gave way and she plunged into the shaft. The flames in the pit roared as they took her.

More explosions ruptured the deck. Finn was still standing, but his seconds were numbered. There was no route for escape. Fire and falling beams blocked his path to the shuttle.

"Finn!" Rose yelled.

She sat with BB-8 in the cockpit head of the bipedal walker, working its controls. It lumbered through the ruined hangar and took a wide step over the pit. Finn scrambled up a leg.

He held on tight as the walker hotfooted it to the shuttle.

After the light, there was darkness. Kylo Ren sank deeper and deeper into it until a sound roused him out of the void. A footstep, followed by a feeling.

He was about to die.

Kylo Ren woke to find General Hux standing over him. Hux's hand swayed from the blaster he was about to pull. His face knitted in false concern. "What happened?"

Ren staggered to his feet. He was still in the throne room, with his slain master and the Praetorians rotting on the floor. Smoke drifted from where Luke's lightsaber had exploded. Rey, however, was nowhere to be seen.

"The girl murdered Snoke," he said.

Bodies slid as the floor suddenly tipped. Hux grabbed

the shreds of a hanging curtain while Ren rooted his feet to the floor. A fiery light poured through the viewport behind the throne.

Ren beheld a cataclysm out in space.

The *Supremacy* had been shorn in two, the innards of its bisected other half visible as explosions tore it further apart. Smaller Destroyers burned around it, their spear-headed bows colliding into each other to feed an expanding chaos.

It was Ren's turn to ask the question. "What happened?"

Hux didn't answer. The room's grav-units reestablished themselves and he rushed to the airlock, accessing its console. He frowned. "Snoke's escape shuttle is gone."

Ren stared into the inferno. Rey was somewhere out there, fleeing in the shuttle. "We know where she's going. Get our forces down to that Resistance base. Let's finish this."

Hux turned from the airlock. "Finish this? You presume to command *my* army?" He challenged Ren with a look of pure disdain. "We have no ruler. The Supreme Leader is dead!"

Ren stepped over the corpse of his master and pinched his fingers, picturing them on Hux's windpipe. The general began to choke.

"The Supreme Leader," Kylo Ren said, "is dead."

Hux sagged before Ren, tugging at his collar as if that could stop the strangulation. "Long . . . live . . ." he rasped, looking up at Ren, "the . . . Supreme Leader."

All glints of challenge vanished from Hux's eyes. Kylo Ren released him to gasp for breath on his knees.

As it had so often in her life, history was repeating itself.

Bundled in a high-collared coat, Leia stared out at the surface of Crait from the entrance of the old rebel fort. Around her loomed a ridge of coal-dark mountains. Behind her, the last soldiers of the Resistance carried out Captain Dameron's orders to arm themselves. And before her stretched a plain as desolate as Hoth's icy wastes, with salt in place of snow. Soon the walkers and war machines of the First Order would trample that ground and wage an assault on the base, just as the Empire had forty years before on the planet Hoth.

The Rebel Alliance had survived that siege, managing to evacuate in time. The Resistance had no such option. All of the six transports that had landed on Crait were damaged and in need of repair. Even if they launched, they would never get far without an ion cannon to neutralize the Destroyers in orbit. Unlike Hoth, the base on Crait wasn't much more than a warren of abandoned mineral mines with a deflector shield and armor-shelled outer door. Leia would transmit a distress call for reinforcements, but if none came by the time the First Order broke through the door, it would all be over.

Perhaps history wasn't repeating itself. Perhaps this was the end.

She reproached herself for having such thoughts. She'd been in similar dead-end situations in the past, and she wasn't dead, not yet. She had to hold on to hope. As she told her troops, if you only believed in the sun when you saw it, you'd never make it through the night.

She touched the beacon on her wrist. Rey was still out there, somewhere, as was Luke. The stimshots and medical droids had bolstered her recovery, but it was her brother who had boosted her strength and saved her from the brink of death.

She looked up at the sky and thought of him.

Six TIE fighters and a First Order assault shuttle broke through the clouds and descended toward the base. It seemed rather small for an advance attack group. The First Order's armada had only been crippled, not destroyed. Nonetheless, she was well aware of the size of the force that would follow.

"They're coming. Shut the door."

She retreated into the base. The shield door, a reinforced block a hundred meters tall, began to drop, its rusty gears whining from years of nonuse. When they had arrived, Leia was grateful that her old rebel codes had opened the door. Now she prayed she wasn't sealing them all in a tomb.

As the Resistance soldiers went farther back into the mines, so did the mountain's native inhabitants, a four-legged species the rebels had called crystal foxes because of the crystalline spines bristling from their vulpine bodies. Whenever the foxes moved, the spines clinked like a symphony of chimes. How and why the foxes had evolved in that way, no one knew. War always put the natural sciences on the backburner.

The First Order shuttle sped ahead of the TIEs and arrowed toward the base's entrance. "Take cover!" Poe yelled.

He ran toward the entrance, firing at the shuttle with a heavy rifle. The shuttle dipped low, beneath the door, losing its upper fin in a close shave. It bounced on the ground, slid, and came to a halt. The shield door boomed shut behind it.

Leia grabbed a rifle and joined Poe, who blasted open the shuttle's canopy. "Don't shoot!" cried someone in the shuttle. "It's us!"

Finn and Rose emerged from the shattered cockpit.

"Finn!" Poe shouted. "You're not dead! Where's my droid?"

Leia lowered her rifle while Poe dropped his and hurried over to his friends. To his delight, BB-8 zoomed down the shuttle's boarding ramp, beeping excitedly. Their reunion was a rare moment of happiness that Leia would've loved to prolong, if there weren't other life-and-death factors involved.

They had to prepare for war. And she had a message to send.

CHAPTER
23

A SUCCESSFUL escape from a disintegrating Mega-Destroyer and a squadron of TIE fighters would normally be cause to celebrate. But not now. As Finn squinted through the periscope for a glimpse outside the shield door, he knew he had fled one battle zone only to enter another.

First Order gunships and troop transports were landing by the dozens on the salt flats outside. Gorilla walkers unfolded from their moorings on the sides of gunships, each step causing the ground to quake. Hovertanks floated down cargo ramps. What worried Finn the most was the appearance of a gargantuan superlaser barrel on rotating treads.

"A battering ram cannon," he told Rose and Poe, who stood around him. "It'll crack this door open like an egg."

Rose looked around the mine's entry chamber. Some of the crystal foxes had returned to watch them with tiny red eyes. "There has to be a back way out of here, right?"

BB-8 zipped up to them, with C-3PO doing his best to keep up. "Beebee-Ate has analyzed the mine schematics. This is the only way in or out, I'm afraid," the droid said.

Finn tried to game out the situation. They were safe from orbital bombardment at the present, since the fort's deflector shield still worked. General Organa had also transmitted her distress message to potential allies, but it would take time for them to respond and send reinforcements.

The walls shook. The army outside was advancing. Finn knew the band of Resistance soldiers who manned the fort's outer trenches would put up a good fight, but they didn't have the numbers or firepower to repel the attackers. Once those defenses were sufficiently weakened, the cannon would be charged and fired. The seismic force of its blast would blow a hole through the shield door, and then stormtroopers would enter and slaughter them all.

Finn saw only one way they could buy time for potential reinforcements. "We have to take out that cannon."

Rey saw stars. And lights. And more stars.

But the stars in the viewport began to fade away, as did the lights on the console. Everything was fading—even the sound of her breathing—into a quiet, dark nothingness.

Stay here. I'll come back for you, sweetheart. I promise.

Jarred by the voice, she sat bolt upright in the cockpit of Snoke's private shuttle. Of course there was no one else in the ship. Those words were just an echo in her mind. Something she had repeated to herself to stay alive on Jakku. A truth about herself with which she had reconciled.

Those words had just saved her, drawing her from what could have been a deadly slumber.

All the cells in Rey's body seemed to pulse in pain. The fight with Snoke and Ben had taken everything she had. When Ben had fallen, she'd managed to retrieve the pieces of Luke's lightsaber and drag herself onto Snoke's shuttle. She had worked up just enough energy to set the autopilot and send a message to R2-D2 before crashing into the pilot's chair.

Alert now, Rey saw the shuttle had navigated through the smash-up of Destroyers. Yet instead of an open starfield, another starship filled the viewport, one familiar to Rey.

The *Millennium Falcon*.

The console buzzed from an incoming signal. Rey opened a channel. Chewbacca's arfs broke through the subspace static. Was she okay?

Rey slipped out of the chair. "I'm alive, if that counts for something. But I'm going to need a medpac."

A tube extended from the *Falcon* and docked with the shuttle. Rey staggered through it onto the freighter. R2-D2 retracted the tube and closed the hatch.

Rey opened a first-aid locker and promptly jumped back. Four porgs tumbled out. They landed on top of each other, then righted themselves and waddled to another clutch. Rey looked around and noticed the stumpy avians were everywhere. They peeked out of the ventilation ducts, nibbled on coolant casings, and even hung upside down from the ceiling conduits. The *Millennium Falcon* had become a circus of porgs!

Over their cooing and chirping, she heard R2-D2 beeping uncontrollably.

"What'd you say?" she said.

The droid repeated the beeps at a volume that made Rey wince. But she understood the binary. While scanning the emergency bands, R2-D2 had picked up a distress call from General Organa.

The Resistance had taken refuge on a nearby planet. And they were at death's door. If they didn't get help soon, the First Order would wipe them out for good.

Forgetting about her pain, Rey hopped over porgs and ran to the cockpit. She wouldn't know what to do with herself if she never saw Finn or her friends again.

Alone on the ledge of her chute, Rose buckled herself in the skimmer. It was a dangerous-looking contraption, more akin to a podracer than a speeder, designed to slalom across flat surfaces with a long mono-ski. From each side of an open cockpit spread a delicate wing that ended in repulsor boosters. Rose had discovered a number of skimmers in the fort's vehicle garage, and though most of them had been gutted for tech, some were in decent enough shape to operate. At the very least, they would give the team the necessary speed to execute Finn's plan to take out the battering ram cannon.

Once settled in the skimmer's seat, Rose slid the goggles over her eyes. The batteries for the internal scopes had long since died, but the tinted lenses would prevent her from being blinded by Crait's stark white surface.

She took a breath, then leapt into the chute.

The skimmer whipped down the tube, gathering speed. Rose revolved on the seat's gimbal, her body spinning with the curves. She felt both giddy and dizzy all at once. Paige would have loved this.

The chute opened ahead and she shot out of a hole in the shield door, soaring high in the air. Finn, Poe, C'ai Threnalli, and nine other pilots and soldiers ejected from adjacent tubes on their own skimmers. They all dropped toward the ground as a pack, engaging their mono-skis. When she noticed that Finn hadn't engaged his, Rose cued him over the comm. He seemed dazed by the plunge, yet right before touching down, he pressed the button and deployed his mono-ski.

The thirteen skimmers landed in a spume of red as the mono-skis dug up crystals that lay beneath the salt. Scarlet clouds of crystal dust trailed them like exhaust fumes as they shot across the surface. Rose brought her skimmer alongside both Finn and Poe, with the others fanning out around them.

A panel popped loose on Poe's skimmer. He pounded it down, venting his frustration over the comm. "I don't like these rust buckets and I don't like our odds. Keep it tight and don't get pulled too close till they roll that cannon out front."

The skimmers darted past the rebel fort's trenches, which were manned by what remained of the Resistance army. TIE fighters crisscrossed above the skimmers while higher in the sky a black folded-wing shuttle circled like a menacing predator. Rose could only guess it contained someone of importance to the First Order.

"Ground forces, lay down some fire!" Poe radioed to the trenches.

The decrepit turbolaser towers and rusted artillery emplacements unloaded on the First Order's advancing front line. The armor on the walkers and tanks absorbed most of the shots, but the barrage provided cover fire for the skimmers to approach.

Rose draped her necklace over the skimmer's controls. It reminded her of why she was fighting—and what was worth dying for. If she could have an ounce of her sister's courage, perhaps she could make an impact.

Her courage was tested immediately. TIEs screamed over them, raining lasers. One of the skimmers fell away in a smear of red.

At Poe's command, the skimmers dispersed and the TIEs broke formation to follow. Rose skated across the flats, banking to the sides as a TIE chased her. The starfighter's guns gouged dark red cracks in the ground.

Rose possessed none of her sister's skill in gunnery, and her potshots went nowhere. Poe and the trench batteries had better luck, and several TIEs went down in flames, including the one chasing her. Yet those losses didn't put much of a dent in the enemy squadron.

"We can't match this firepower!" Threnalli yelled over the comm.

"We've gotta hold them till they pull out the cannon!" Poe snapped back.

More skimmers met their end, picked off by TIEs in succession. Their crashes gashed the ground as if the land itself bled. Worse yet, the defensive fire from the turbolaser batteries had all but stopped. TIEs swarmed over the trenches, spitting death at the Resistance soldiers and knocking out artillery.

The battle was turning into a massacre.

Rose looked at her medallion. She remembered her homeworld of Otomok, her friends in the Resistance, her sister. They were worth fighting for and they were also worth dying for.

She gripped her control sticks and rocketed toward the front lines.

"Rose! Behind you!" Finn cried out.

She glanced back as a trio of TIEs dove at her skimmer. Their laser cannons glowed, about to be triggered. It was over for her.

She flinched as all three TIEs were blasted from behind.

A Corellian freighter, which looked as banged-up as anything else from the fort, soared through the fiery wreckage. Rose gaped at the ship, barely keeping control of her skimmer. Had she just been saved by the *Millennium Falcon*?

"Yeah!" Finn whooped.

The *Falcon* looped around and went right back at the TIEs, blowing the wings and cockpits off two more. Like a school of gutterguppies, the TIEs veered away from the skimmers in pursuit of the freighter.

Rose smiled and closed ranks with the other skimmers.

"She drew them all off!" Poe said over the comm. "All of them!"

The *Falcon* made an abrupt drop into a crevice, a move most of the TIEs failed in spectacular fashion. Some smashed into the surface, others into the sides of the crevice, and all went up in flames.

"Oh, they hate that ship." Finn's voice crackled over the comm.

Rose refocused her attention on the front lines, which started to open. "There it is," she said, feeling the ground rumble.

Two multi-legged tug walkers plodded forward, yoked to the battering ram cannon. Plated in dense armor, the mammoth siege gun that was dragged forward seemed even more imposing than Finn had described—perhaps fifty meters tall, nearly half the height of the shield door.

"Our only shot is right down the throat," Finn said.

Rose studied the cannon. Its grooved head began to warm up, pulsing with the energy of its superlaser. To aim a shot down the giant barrel, they'd have to fly straight up to the cannon, which was going to be nearly impossible with the First Order forces protecting it.

Poe led the way. "Hold tight!"

The turbolaser towers that had outlasted the TIEs

renewed the assault. The walkers and hovertanks responded in kind, peppering the trenches with their guns. But when the black command shuttle dropped lower and started targeting the skimmers, the rest of the First Order's forces did the same, concentrating their fire.

Rose managed to evade the lasers, but the skimmer beside hers didn't. After the cloud from its crash cleared, Rose saw that the battering ram cannon held a steady, deadly glow.

"All craft pull away!" Poe said. "The gun's charged. It's a suicide run!"

Rose inverted her skimmer, eluding another blast, and steered clear of the lasers, following Poe and the others back to the trenches. But Finn kept speeding toward the cannon. "I'm almost there!" he said over the comm.

"Retreat—that's an order!" Poe barked. "To the trenches!"

Finn wasn't listening. He sideslipped his skimmer through the cannon fire, dusting up more crystalline clouds. Though he claimed to be a terrible pilot, the ex-stormtrooper's deft maneuvering was nothing short of astounding.

Finn's flying was inspired.

But Rose knew that an errant blaster bolt was all it would take to cause her friend to crash and burn. "Finn, it's too late!" she screamed into her headset. "Don't do this!"

"I won't let them win, Rose," Finn said.

"No! Finn, listen—"

His comm signature crackled off and he accelerated toward the cannon. Its barrel shone through the lasers, on the cusp of firing. The tremendous heat it generated melted the salt around it, stirring a crimson haze around its treads. With the other skimmers no longer a threat, all the walkers and tanks were targeting Finn. And Rose knew he'd never get through that last stretch alive.

She glanced at her medallion dangling from the controls. If there was anyone in the universe worth fighting for—anyone worth dying for—it was someone like Finn.

Rose tacked away from Poe and rocketed toward her friend.

Enemy fire pummeled Finn's skimmer, blowing off pieces. Flames licked his cockpit. Somehow his craft continued toward the cannon barrel—until Rose crashed into him from behind.

She hit his boosters, causing his skimmer to bank and roll off its mono-ski. One of his wings bashed into the ground and his cockpit skidded across the salt in a spray of red.

The shot cost Rose control of her craft. She couldn't see in the cloud of dust, and her skimmer spun on its mono-ski. There was a screech of metal, then her dashboard crumpled and her ribs crunched against the crash buckle.

When she came to her senses, Finn held her in his arms. She realized she was hurt, yet she couldn't feel any pain. The wreckage of their skimmers smoldered around them.

Tears rimmed Finn's eyes. "Why did you stop me?"

She found the air to speak. "*Saved* you, dummy," she said, coughing. "That's how we're going to win. Not fighting what we hate, but saving what we love."

The cannon's blast shook the world. Rose didn't need to see the impact to know the shield door wouldn't hold.

Nor could she hold back her feelings.

Lifting her head, she kissed Finn.

CHAPTER
24

LEIA had never been so dismayed to see the sun. The light that streamed through the cracked shield door boded only doom. Soon stormtroopers would flood into the fort by the thousands, and there wouldn't be any reinforcements to save them. No one had replied to her distress signal.

The First Order had won.

"We fought to the end," Leia told those assembled in the fort's small command center. "But the galaxy has lost its hope. The spark is out."

Faces fell, hers with them. Leia's younger self, that fierce princess, would have berated her for giving such a speech. But she was older now, wiser, not blinded by the passions of youth. And she was tired. The relentlessness of war had worn her down. It seemed like no matter what she did, anything she ever loved the galaxy saw fit to take away. She had fought the good fight, yes, but in the end it hadn't been enough.

Perhaps that was the ultimate lesson of life. To love is to lose.

Footsteps echoed in the cavern. Were the stormtroopers here so soon? She lifted her head.

A man in tattered black robes stood before her.

Leia blinked a couple of times, fearing she was hallucinating. But if she was, it was a mass hallucination, because the Resistance officers in the command center shared her surprise. The man pulled back his hood, revealing the lined, bearded face of her twin.

"Luke . . ." she breathed.

"Master Luke!" C-3PO's excitement nearly fried his vocabulator.

Luke acknowledged the droid with a nod and walked to his sister. He sat down across from her.

"I know what you're gonna say," Leia said with a slight smile. "I changed my hair."

"It looks nice that way," he said with a smile of his own.

She didn't comment on *his* hair. It was shaggy and needed a scrub. But that had little bearing in the grand scheme of things.

"Leia . . . I'm sorry."

There had been times over the years when Leia wanted to lash out at him for disappearing when she—and the galaxy—needed him most. But she felt none of that anger now, and she was too exhausted to scold him. Just seeing her brother one last time was enough.

"I know," she said. "I know you are. I'm just glad you're here, at the end."

They had entered life together as twins, and now, as twins, they would leave it. Yet the fact that he had rejoined Leia after so long stirred some embers inside her.

"This *is* the end . . . isn't it?" she asked.

Luke's eyes had a strange glint. "I came to face him, Leia. And I can't save him."

"I held out hope for so long." Leia shook her head. "My son is gone."

The glint in Luke's eyes seemed even stranger. "No one's ever really gone," he said.

That was the old Luke talking, the Luke she'd once known who could discern even the dimmest light in the darkest of hearts. He had found a way to redeem a man she never could—their father. If Luke couldn't save Ben, maybe he believed someone else could.

Leia placed her hand on top of his and her weariness faded away. When at last Luke withdrew his hand, she held in hers a pair of chance cubes—Han's dice, which he'd hung in the cockpit of the *Millennium Falcon*. Luke must have taken them from the *Falcon*, meaning he must have met Rey. Might he have taught her something? Could the girl from Jakku somehow help them all—even Ben?

Leia smiled. Maybe the Resistance—and the galaxy—still had a chance.

In the cockpit of his command shuttle, Kylo Ren watched the First Order's army march across the salt flats to the rebel fort. The battering ram cannon had punched through the shield door, where a sunbeam shone on the hole like a celestial spotlight.

Everything had fallen in place. He had destroyed his odious master, and now he would do the same to the vile Resistance.

A lone figure wearing dark robes emerged from the crack in the door. At first, he thought it was a Resistance messenger, coming to make a last-ditch negotiation he'd never accept. But as the figure walked through the sunbeam, Ren realized it was not a messenger, but his master—his *former* master.

"Stop."

Standing beside Ren, General Hux seemed puzzled by the order but gestured to his officers in the cockpit that it be transmitted to all ground forces. The walkers, hovertanks, and troopers came to a halt, still some distance from the fort.

Skywalker strode across the red-stained salt flats, his robes frayed and flapping, like some crazy beggar on a fool's errand. The hundreds of stormtrooper rifles, walker guns, and hovertank cannons pointed at him did not give him the slightest pause. He stopped below where the shuttle hovered, and with the wind whipping his unruly hair, he looked up to the cockpit and stared at Ren through the transparisteel canopy.

Ren trembled and immediately admonished himself for it. Why should he fear this madman? Skywalker was old and weak. His influence in the galaxy had faded like a burnt-out star.

"Supreme Leader, shall we advance?" General Hux asked.

Ren kept his gaze locked on Skywalker. "I want every gun we have to fire on that man." When Hux hesitated, Ren snarled, "Do it."

Hux nodded and relayed the command. One trigger-happy gunner in an AT-M6 walker fired first, initiating a megacaliber barrage that enveloped Skywalker in a column of fire.

"More," Ren said.

Hux cocked an eyebrow at Ren. "We've surely—"

"More!"

The shuttle opened fire, along with every gun below, making a crater where Skywalker stood. When smoke and salt jeopardized their sensor arrays, Hux took over. "Enough—*enough*!" The officers frantically issued the order and the firing petered out.

Hux turned to the shuttle's commander. "You think you got him?" he said sarcastically.

The man nodded, though visual confirmation was difficult with all the smoke. Ren slumped into a seat, breathing hard. His mouth, his eyes were wet. His gloved hands ached from clenching his fists too tightly.

"Now, if we're ready to get moving, we can finish this," Hux said.

The shuttle commander swallowed loudly. "Sir . . ."

An unnerving silence fell over the bridge. Ren followed Hux's incredulous stare outside the shuttle.

Luke Skywalker climbed out of the crater, showing no sign of injury. He swept dust off his robes and raised his eyes to meet Ren's again.

Rage surged through Ren. He rose from his seat. "Bring me down to him. And don't advance our forces until I say."

"Supreme Leader, don't be distracted," Hux said, exasperated. "Our goal is to kill the Resistance. They're helpless in the mine, but every moment we waste—"

Ren waved his hand and Hux was tossed into the bulkhead.

The shuttle commander's swallow was even louder this time. "Right away, sir." He had the pilot land the ship on the battlefield. Ren left the cockpit and went to the hatch.

He ran his hand along his lightsaber hilt before he disembarked. Though he didn't know what trick his former master might be pulling, when the opportunity presented itself, Ren would strike him down once and for all.

Skywalker waited for Ren on the battlefield. The crater behind him flickered with flames.

"Old man," Ren jeered. "Did you come back to say you forgive me? To save my soul, like my father?"

"No."

Skywalker's bluntness came as no surprise to Kylo Ren. This was not the heroic Skywalker whom everyone admired. This was the villainous Skywalker who had tried to murder Ren in his sleep.

Kylo Ren ignited his lightsaber.

———

At the behest of General Organa, Poe had spent months scouring the galaxy for clues to the whereabouts of Luke Skywalker. It had been a frustrating assignment, full of dead ends, and he often doubted anything would come of it. But now all his hard work had borne a most marvelous fruit.

Luke Skywalker had appeared on the battlefield.

The First Order's forces turned their guns away from the trenches and fired at Luke. Poe knew it would be folly to assist the Jedi. If Luke survived, it would be because of the powers he was rumored to have, not anything Poe could do. But in the meantime, the First Order was distracted, and the smoke from its fusillade provided the ideal cover for retreat.

Poe parked his skimmer and jumped out. Screaming at the top of his lungs, he ordered the Resistance troops out of the trenches and back into the mine. One soldier was too injured to run, so Poe threw an arm around her shoulder and helped her along.

Before reentering the mine, Poe glanced back at where Finn and Rose had crashed. But he could see nothing through a curtain of dense black smoke.

Finn stripped wire from his skimmer. The smoke had drifted past, so he could inhale without worry. But his lips tingled strangely, probably from the salt in the air.

Or was it from Rose's kiss?

She lay on a metal sheet he'd torn off the skimmer. He corded the wire around her waist and her legs so she wouldn't slip off. The leftover wire he used to rope the skimmer's laser barrels through the holes he'd punched into the sides of the sheeting. He then lifted both barrel ends and started to pull Rose on his improvised sled.

The going was tough, the ground slippery. Finn had to take a longer route back to the mine, to avoid the thickest patches of smoke. Whenever they were out in the open, Finn dreaded the seemingly inevitable laser barrage. Yet for some reason, the gorilla walkers ignored them.

He checked on Rose periodically. She moaned at times, a sign she was still alive. It kept him pulling. So did his thoughts of Rey. If the *Millennium Falcon* had come to Crait, surely she was flying it. And as long as she piloted that ship, a rescue didn't seem out of the question.

When they neared the trenches, Rose whimpered something. He looked down at her. "What's that?"

A smile bloomed across her dirty cheeks. "When we met, I was dragging you," she whispered. "Now you're dragging me."

He snickered, remembering how this feisty maintenance tech had wanted to turn him in as a deserter. "We've come a long way, haven't we?"

Around the turbolaser towers, only the dead remained. The surviving soldiers were fleeing through the crack in the base's shield door. Finn and Rose would be there soon, once they crossed the trenches.

"Who's that?" Rose asked.

She pointed across the plain. The First Order walkers

had halted before a hooded figure. Smoke coiled from the crater behind him.

Finn had an inkling who the figure might be, but he didn't waste time confirming. Rose's life depended on getting into the mine.

After taking the wounded to a medic, Poe ran into the small command bunker inside the rebel base. General Organa stood before a blank screen, lost in thought.

"General, all survivors have returned," he said. "I advise we set up a heavy cannon and blast anyone else who comes through that crack. And I believe your brother—"

"What about your friends?"

"Finn?" Poe swallowed. Just saying his buddy's name—a name he'd personally given the ex-stormtrooper—felt like a shot in the gut. "He . . . didn't make it."

She turned from the screen. "Are you sure about that, Commander Dameron?"

He blinked, unsure of what to say. Was she questioning what had happened out there? And had she just reinstated his rank?

He followed her gaze out the bunker, toward the entrance of the mine, where he witnessed the day's second miracle.

"Finn!"

His friend clambered through the crack in the shield door, hoisting Rose on a makeshift sled. "Medpac! I need a medpac here!" Finn shouted.

Some soldiers got there before Poe, taking the sled out of Finn's arms and carrying Rose to the bunker. Finn glanced out the crack in the door as Poe ran toward him. "Was that—"

"I think, yeah." Poe peered into the periscope for a glimpse outside. Two figures in black confronted each other on the battlefield, one brandishing a red lightsaber, the other igniting a blue blade. The man who held the blue blade was indeed Luke, as he had thought. The other, however, was the brutal fiend who had tortured Poe on the *Finalizer*. "Kylo Ren—Luke's facing him alone."

"We should help him," Finn insisted. "Let's go!" Poe turned from the periscope. The few able-bodied soldiers left looked at him for their new orders. They'd run back out there if he asked them. But Luke hadn't asked for anyone's help. "No no no. We are the spark that'll light the fire that'll burn down the First Order. He's stalling him so we can escape."

Finn's jaw dropped. "Escape? He's one man against an army! We have to go help him!"

Leia walked out of the bunker, C-3PO clanking behind her. She glanced at Poe, saying nothing. Her look told him to not to stop.

"No," Poe said. "Luke's doing this so we can survive. There has to be another way out of this mine. Heck, how'd he get in?"

C-3PO lent his expertise. "Sir, it is possible that a natural unmapped opening exists. But this facility is such a maze of endless tunnels, that the odds of finding an exit are—"

Poe shushed the droid. "Shut up."

"—fifteen thousand, four hundred twenty-eight—"

"Shut up!"

"—to one," Threepio finished.

Poe stared into one of the mine's tunnels. He saw nothing in the darkness and, moreover, *heard* nothing.

Finn voiced what Poe was thinking. "Where'd the crystal critters go?"

There was something—a pair of red eyes blinking back at them. Then the fox scampered deeper into the tunnel, its spines tinkling.

"Follow me," Poe said.

Everyone turned to General Organa as if waiting for an order. "What are you looking at me for? Follow him," she said.

She stepped behind Poe, the first to abide by his instructions.

CHAPTER
25

REY swatted a porg away from the mapping scopes while Chewbacca glided the *Millennium Falcon* over a crystal glacier. More porgs fluttered around the cockpit but she ignored them. A dot blinked steadily on the topographic readout, indicating they were near the beacon linked to the one she wore on her wrist. Yet Crait's surface was devoid of anything except salt and mineral deposits.

"The beacon's right beneath this—they've gotta be somewhere," Rey told a discouraged R2-D2. The droid was jacked into the *Falcon*'s sensor systems and hadn't detected any biological signatures other than the porg that had tried to build a nest atop his dome.

"Keep scanning for life-forms." Rey wished she could reach out herself. But the fight had left her body bruised, her mind foggy. And her connection to the Force felt distant, out of tune, as if she had been stretched to her limits.

One thing was clear to her. She was not going to give up on her friends in the Resistance, wherever they were. They needed her help, that much she could sense.

The *Falcon* turned for another pass over the glacier. Rey followed a long gash in the surface to a mountain ridge, scanning, searching, hoping. A porg perched on the dashboard looked out with her.

R2-D2 wobbled and beeped, scaring some of the porgs. The one on the dashboard squawked so loud Rey's eardrums hurt. But then she spotted the reason for R2-D2's excitement. "Chewie, there!"

She pointed to the top of the ridge, where fox-like creatures were dashing out of the mountain in droves. The spines that covered their bodies glinted in the setting sun like icicles.

Despite no sign of her friends, Rey was convinced they were there. Chewbacca landed the *Falcon*, and Rey ran out. She wasn't looking where she was going and fell, sliding down a slope. The last of the spiny creatures jumped past her to join its pack on the ridge above.

The hole the foxes had emerged from was small, no bigger than the length of Rey's hand. It wasn't a crack in the mountain rock itself but, rather, a space between boulders that had been fused together.

A mountain she wouldn't be able to move. But boulders— those she had experience with.

She closed her eyes, exhaled, inhaled, exhaled again. The Force tingled, almost imperceptibly, but she didn't worry. She knew it was there, as it always was. And she trusted that she was part of it.

———

Jedi wisdom held that it was the masters who learned and the students who taught. As he faced his old pupil, Luke understood just how true that was.

Anger swirled around his nephew like a cyclone. It was an anger spurred by distrust and disappointment, expectation and entitlement. Ben Solo had been a child born of privilege, son of a revered princess and a notorious scoundrel, and gifted with a remarkable aptitude in the Force. Nonetheless, given all those things, he wanted something of his own—a name. And he achieved it by rejecting his parents and uncle, by embracing his anger and doing harm to himself and all those around him.

In Kylo Ren, Luke saw the shadow of his own father as a young man—and what he himself could have become if he had not been allowed to grow up as a farm boy on Tatooine.

The young man shifted his weight from one foot to another, his eyes sunken and dark. His gaze was fierce, daring Luke to make the first move.

Luke did not let himself be lured. Patience was another lesson he'd learned from his students.

His nephew charged. Luke slipped out of the way and turned. Both rooted their feet and met the other's stare. Drifting flakes of salt and ash sizzled on their blades.

In the dark pools of his nephew's eyes, Luke was struck by the sight of his own reflection—an old man, grim and tired and sad. "I failed you, Ben. I'm sorry."

"I'm sure you are. The Resistance is dead. The war is over. And when I kill you, I'll have killed the last Jedi."

But reflections are just reflections, they need not be reality. Luke looked past his reflection, past those dark eyes, into the Force.

"Every word of what you just said was wrong," he said to Ben. "The Rebellion is reborn today."

The Force showed him a vision of Rey, who stood at the bottom of a crevasse, meditating as he had taught her. Her hand rose, and so did a stack of boulders, loosened from a hole in a mountain.

"The war is just beginning," Luke said.

Rey's hand twitched. Her breathing changed. Luke sensed she knew he was there with her. He'd always be there.

"And I will not be the last Jedi," Luke said.

Finn watched the boulders levitate from the mouth of the tunnel to reveal Rey, standing on the other side like the last beam of the sunset.

She opened her eyes, teetering. The boulders dropped to the ground. Finn ran to her and took her in his arms. He held her tight. She smiled.

Rey—he had found her again—*Rey!*

But when their eyes met, he saw she wasn't the same Rey he had known.

"*Rey*," Kylo Ren said, snarling her name. "She made her choice. She aligned herself with the old way that has to die. I will destroy her and you and all of it. Know that."

He swung but Skywalker would not cross blades. His former master kept ducking, dipping, evading, eluding. Ren gnashed his teeth, frustrated. But it became clear that Skywalker had to dodge because he could not match Ren's power. Soon he would make a wrong move. And once that happened, Ren would strike him down just as he had struck down Snoke.

"Strike me down in anger," Skywalker said, "and I'll always be with you. Just like your father." He stepped back and deactivated his lightsaber.

That was Skywalker, always trying to lecture, always try to impart his nonsense. This lesson would be his last.

Ren lunged and swung at his master with all his strength, all his rage.

His blade cut nothing but air.

He swung again, and yet again his lightsaber slashed straight through Skywalker. His old master shimmered, as if he wasn't there, as if he was just a hologram, a phantom, a projection of Kylo Ren's mind. What Jedi trick was this?

"See you around, kid," Skywalker said, then vanished.

Ren fumed. He had been goaded by a ghost. And now the trenches were vacant. The Resistance soldiers had fled into the mines. Skywalker had tried to distract him to give them time to get away.

Ren would not let that happen.

He called a squad of troopers to his side and stormed through the shattered shield door into the rebel fort.

The Resistance soldiers weren't in the mines, either. The entrance chamber was empty, as was the command center.

Ren's hand began to tremble. The stormtroopers hurried away from him. He examined the antiquated command center consoles.

He picked up two small objects from the ground. A pair of chance cubes, strung together. Ren knew the dice well. They had been Han's, hanging in the cockpit of—

The *Millennium Falcon*. Ren glimpsed the ship through the Force. Rey and Leia were boarding. Both seemed upset by something.

Rey turned her head in his direction and glared at him. She was angry at him. She thought he had betrayed the person he should be.

But she was wrong. *She* had betrayed *him*.

The *Falcon*'s ramp rose, and Kylo Ren's communion with her ended. He stood alone in the command center, seething with rage. The dice had disappeared, just part of Skywalker's trick.

This time, Leia didn't interrupt any happy reunions. She joined one herself, entering the *Falcon*'s lounge where most of the Resistance's survivors sat. She gave Chewbacca the biggest hug she could, and the Wookiee in turn gathered up everyone else he could in his arms, squeezing the air out of Poe.

Some couldn't partake in the festivities. Rose lay on the

medbed, injured but in a restful sleep, and Finn scrounged in the locker underneath it. Of the many things he pulled out was a set of leather-bound tomes. They looked very old, and Leia wondered how they had come onto the *Falcon*. Han hadn't exactly been a bookworm.

Finn found a blanket and draped it over Rose. Leia noticed Rey seemed puzzled by Finn's attention to the other girl. She distracted herself by inspecting two chrome pieces in her hand.

Leia walked over with a warm smile. Rey returned it, briefly, and showed Leia the halves of Luke's lightsaber. "Luke Skywalker is gone. I felt it," she said, trying to fit the pieces of the hilt together. "But it wasn't sadness or pain. It was peace. And purpose."

"I felt it, too." Leia had sensed Luke's passing, but it hadn't carried the shock of her husband's death or the same weight of grief. Rather, Leia felt that her brother was, as Rey had said, at peace.

Rey stopped fiddling with the lightsaber and looked at Leia. "Kylo is stronger than ever. He has an army and an iron grip on the galaxy. How do we build a rebellion from this?"

Leia took Rey's hand. "We have everything we need."

It was true. The heroes around Leia had renewed her faith. With or without her, they would defend all that was good in the galaxy, as she had tried so hard to do herself.

Her fight—her life—had not been in vain.

EPILOGUE

ONCE there was a boy who grew up to become a Jedi Knight. Not just any Jedi, but one of the greatest in their history. A hero, a warrior, a scholar, and a master.

This Jedi sat on a ledge atop a lonely mountain, his legs crossed beneath him, his eyes closed, a ring of pebbles hovering around him. His mind was returning from another world, where he had fought a great battle, to reunite with his body that had remained on this world, still and silent.

For ordinary beings, the ability to be in two places at once might seem impossible. Yet for a master of the Force, all things were possible. The mind was not limited by the body, nor the body by the mind. The body might even wither and die while the mind and the spirit survived.

This Jedi had not moved since dawn. During that time, the mountain had quaked. A cliff had crumbled. The twin suns had begun to set. The moon had gone on the rise.

It had taken all his strength to do what he had done. The salt lines of tears on his face showed the incredible strain. Now that it was done, he could enjoy a few last breaths from the island that had been his home.

Luke Skywalker was about to die. But it was something he accepted. Death was the way of all things, even the stars.

A pebble from the ring dropped. Then another. And another. Some rolled down the side of the mountain. Others rested on the ledge. His body crumpled to lie with them.

Petals blown by the wind brushed across his robes. The deep fissures in his face relaxed. The twin suns set over the calm seas. And with a last breath, his body faded from the stone, his mind faded into the Force, and his spirit went to walk the skies.

So passed the life of Luke Skywalker. But death would not be the end. His name, his deeds, his legend would live on, reenacted by scrawny stable boys brandishing broomsticks or dreamed about by restless orphan girls who scavenged their barren homes for scraps of hope.

For all things are possible in the Force.